liquididea press

Praise for
The Case of the Wilted Broccoli

"I liked the book a lot! Out of all of the books I have read this is the best one!"

    —*Luka* (Age 8)

"I really like this story."

    —*Jeremy* (Age 10)

"The kids loooooooove it."

    —*Katrina,* mom of Daphne (Age 8) and Zucca (Age 6)

CHILDREN'S BOOKS BY WILL HERTLING

The Case of the Wilted Broccoli

NOVELS FOR TEENS AND ADULTS
BY WILLIAM HERTLING

Avogadro Corp:
The Singularity is Closer than it Appears

A.I. Apocalypse

The Last Firewall

For more information, visit www.williamhertling.com

THE CASE OF THE WILTED BROCCOLI

THE CASE OF THE WILTED BROCCOLI

WILL HERTLING

liquididea press

PORTLAND, OREGON

Copyright © 2014 by William Hertling
ISBN for Paperback: 978-0-9847557-9-0

Cover illustration by M. S. Corley, www.mscorley.com

Keywords: mystery; detective; food supply; middle grade; elementary school; drones; quadcopter; school, cafeteria; Portland, Oregon; science fair project; amateur sleuth; escape; spy camera; investigation; warehouse; drone; deduction; stolen broccoli; food poisoning; adolescent; technology; science fiction; wrist watch; binoculars; laptop computer; police; interrogation; jail; delivery; cell phone; city bus.

For Gifford, Luc, and Rowan

CHAPTER ONE

The weirdness started at lunch on Monday, but Willow didn't discover that until a few weeks later.

Willow was in the fifth grade at Mt. Hood Elementary School in Portland, Oregon. She had two brothers, Elon and Linden, fraternal twins that looked different from each other. They were all named for trees, because that's the sort of thing people did in Portland.

Willow said *sayōnara* to her Japanese teacher, Akiyama Sensei. After lunch she'd go to English. In her school, half the day was taught in Japanese and half in English.

She got to the cafeteria and sought out her best friend, Atlanta, who waited by the hot lunch line. Basil joined them too, getting in line behind Willow, receiving and ignoring a dirty look from the kids he cut.

"Hey," he said.

Boys were so eloquent.

"Hay is for horses, Basil. Good afternoon to you," Willow said, with a slight smirk, looking down at Basil. The second tallest student in the school, she looked down at nearly everyone.

The three had been friends since their first-grade class together. Basil's name, pronounced BAH-zell, had been the subject of many food jokes when they were younger.

Atlanta and Willow chose teriyaki beef and broccoli, and Basil slid a peanut butter and jelly sandwich onto his tray, the same thing he picked every day.

Bringing their lunch to a table, they planned their science-fair projects as they ate, trying to ignore a group of unruly fourth graders at the next table. A straw rose up from the crowd and Willow yelled "Dang it!" and ducked.

A spitball flew harmlessly over her head, landing in Basil's plate. He glared at the fourth graders, then sighed and hunkered down low with the girls.

"I want to do a hair-braiding project for the science fair," Atlanta said, "and make ropes strong enough to hold someone."

"Wicked," Basil said. "With a long enough rope, like twelve feet or so, you could make a swing people could use! That'd be the most popular project."

"Yeah, cool," Willow said. "But, where would you get enough hair? I mean, my braid probably is strong enough to hold a person, but it's not even a foot long."

"Other kids would give us their hair," Atlanta said, "and after the science fair, we'll donate what we collect to make wigs for people who don't have any."

"Brilliant! They have an organization that collects hair for people with cancer," Basil said. "Can I help?"

"Sure," Atlanta said.

Willow doubted the feasibility of their plan to donate the hair. Even if kids contributed their hair, and Basil and Atlanta successfully made a giant braid, how would they separate the mixed hair back into the right sets for donation? She couldn't imagine people wanting wigs with a mix of hair colors. But one glance at Basil's and Atlanta's faces was enough to see they were excited. They'd got bummed if she brought up all the reasons it wouldn't work, so she smiled and kept quiet.

"Awesome," Basil said. "I'll set up a stand by the main entrance with scissors and cut kids hair when they come to school." He turned to Willow. "Can I have yours?"

"What? No way!" She took a quick glance at her brown braid. It'd taken years to grow out to this length. She glanced at Atlanta, whose short blonde hair would be of no help.

"You're in too, right?" Basil asked.

"Nah, I'm doing a project with Elon and Linden," Willow said.

"Your brothers?" they cried out in unison.

"Yeah, Elon wants to build an autonomous drone." Though Willow loved her brothers, it could sometimes be challenging for all three of them to get along. Elon had convinced them the drone would be the best science fair project ever, but the only way they'd get it done was to work together. And Willow wanted to win.

"A what?" Basil asked.

"An autonomous drone. An airplane that flies itself and takes pictures to send to your phone or computer."

Basil glanced back and forth between Willow and Atlanta, obviously thinking that a self-flying plane sounded way cooler than hair braiding and trying to figure out how to renege on his participation with Atlanta.

Atlanta saw this and stared hard at Basil, challenging him to go back on his word.

His shoulders slumped a little and he managed a weak smile. "Let me know if you need any help. Maybe I can find some time."

"When you're not braiding hair," Atlanta reminded him.

"Yeah, then." Basil went back to his sandwich.

Poor Basil. The drone might become the coolest science fair project ever done at Mt. Hood Elementary.

After lunch, they studied reptiles in Mrs. Dozen's

class during the English portion of their day. Their teacher had brought in her pet snake for the month, a not-too-surprising occurrence. So far this year she'd produced a parrot (disruptive to class), a rabbit (surprisingly smelly), a chicken (pooped everywhere), a turtle (tripping hazard), and a ferret (it bit). Willow tried to imagine Mrs. Dozen's house, but what came to mind was the Oregon Zoo. How could all these animals coexist in someone's house?

They'd been waiting all week to feed the snake, a six-foot-long Brazilian rainbow boa constrictor. Today Mrs. Dozen had a mouse squeaking in a box on her desk, and the class tried to concentrate on her lecture, but the snake smell had the mouse shrieking in dire fear.

Willow's stomach turned flips, but not because of the snake. Even though the idea of the snake eating a mouse grossed out a few of her classmates, Willow was interested in watching. She couldn't imagine how a whole mouse would fit into such a slender body. No, her stomach hurt for some other reason and the feeling kept getting worse.

"Ready, class?" Mrs. Dozen called out. "Assemble quietly around Mr. E. Shorter people in front please."

Everyone rushed for the cage, and Basil hurdled a table to get near the front.

"Class," Mrs. Dozen said in a voice that somehow was and wasn't a yell at the same time.

5

They all froze.

"If we rush towards Mr. E, he'll get scared and won't eat. Please walk like a ninja."

The students resumed, tiptoeing, Basil still in front, somehow. A few kids hung back, and Natalie had her eyes covered.

Mrs. Dozen reached in and extracted the mouse. Willow wrapped her arms around her now-grumbling stomach, a slight sweat breaking out on her forehead.

Mrs. Dozen held the squeaking and wriggling cute little guy firmly in one hand. There were a few "oohs" and "aahs" near the front, and a solitary "oh, gross."

"Um, Mrs. Dozen, can I use the restroom?" Atlanta said, one hand up.

"Right now?" Mrs. Dozen said, the mouse dangling over the cage.

"Yes, it's an emergency."

Mrs. Dozen sighed. "Fine, go ahead, but I'm not waiting."

"Thank you," Atlanta said, and rushed for the door.

Everyone tightly packed into three concentric rings with Mrs. Dozen, the mouse, and the snake at the epicenter.

The class collectively held their breath as Mrs. Dozen brought the mouse closer to the cage.

Willow's stomach rumbled again, and she thought she might need to fart. Or maybe poop. Or maybe throw up. The sweat came a little faster on her fore-head.

"Mrs. Dozen," Willow said, holding one hand up as she held her stomach with the other. "I really need to go to the bathroom, too."

"No way, Jose," she said. "You and Atlanta can't go at the same time."

It's true, Mrs. Dozen made this rule halfway through the year, when Atlanta and Willow took a little bit too long of a trip. Maybe forty minutes too long, an escapade eventually requiring the vice principal, custodian, and gym teacher to track them down.

"I, uh, really need to go."

"Not till Atlanta comes back," she said, never taking her eyes off the cage.

Everyone pushed in a little more as Mrs. Dozen slow-ly let the mouse down. The little rodent ran around the circumference of the rectangular tank two or three times, whiskers going crazy, then froze when it saw the snake. It dashed frantically for a hiding spot, trying but failing to scurry under a rock.

Mr. E, dormant in one corner until now, stuck out his tongue, which flickered in a blur. His head raised as his body uncoiled and he slowly turned in the direction of the mouse.

Tightly packed in, Willow found herself in the midst of three rows of her classmates, Basil in front to her right, and at least nine kids surrounding her. Her stomach surged once more. OMG, she was going to throw up. She needed to get out, permission or not. She tried to push her way out of the crowd, but everyone crammed in, trying to see better.

She opened her mouth to scream that she needed to get out immediately, but instead of words, what came out was a stream of yellow vomit. As she realized what was happening, she struggled harder to push her way out. But she kept throwing up as she turned around, chunks of teriyaki beef and broccoli flying out. Everyone else screamed and scattered to get away as she finally broke free and stumbled toward the wastebasket.

Leaning over the garbage pail, her stomach heaved, and for a moment she couldn't think of anything, though she heard a hubbub behind her. The cramping gradually subsided, and she glanced back to the sight of the whole class staring at her.

Well, everyone except for the half-dozen who were freaking out. In the tight-packed crowd, she'd somehow managed to hit Nicolas (in front of her), Basil (front-right), Alice (right), Caden (behind-right), and Emma (behind), before finally breaking free. Still other kids stood in a yellowish puddle, lifting first one foot, and then the other, unsure of what to do. Nancy picked a piece of broccoli off her shirt.

She weakly pointed toward the cage. "Look!" But it was too late. Mr. E had swallowed the mouse and no one saw it, because they were all watching her.

She wanted to disappear from planet Earth.

CHAPTER TWO

Linden and Bobby snuck up behind Elon and Kazuki, who were playing wall ball. Linden mimed pulling out his lightsaber as Bobby did the same, and they attacked in unison from behind, Linden slashing sideways as he made the saber-cutting noise.

Elon and Kazuki startled at first, then caught on instantly, ducking and twisting, pulling out their own sabers and using the Force to hold Linden back.

In a fierce series of blocks and counterstrikes, the battle continued until Kazuki called out, "Got you!"

"No," Linden yelled, "Bobby blocked you."

Kazuki stared into empty space. "Oh, right, sorry

about that." He turned and fought a wicked one-on-one battle against Bobby only he could see, while Linden and his twin-brother, Elon, cheered them on.

Bobby was the fourth member of their group. They had invented him two years ago, in the first grade, when they started turning in homework assignments for him. Their first grade teacher caught on pretty quick, and she'd even grade and return his homework and call on him in class. Of course, he never answered. Gradually word got around, and most of the school knew about Bobby now. He even won a perfect attendance award last year from the principal.

After recess, sweaty from the playground, they walked back to the third-grade classroom. Linden stuffed his lunchbox into his backpack, but Elon was hot lunch, so he walked into class empty-handed.

They took their seats in the Japanese classroom for the afternoon.

"*Gakusei kon'nichiwa. Chakuseki sa sete kudasai,*" their teacher called out.

"*Kon'nichiwa,*" the kids replied in unison, taking their seats as instructed and saying hello.

Elon, sitting one table over, rubbed his stomach and whispered, "I don't feel so good," to Linden.

"Go to the office then," Linden said, glancing over at him.

Elon nodded.

While the teacher handed out papers, Linden forgot about Elon and started to think about their science-fair project. Elon wanted to build an electric self-flying airplane. The science-fair committee had been doubtful they could do it. But the three siblings demonstrated the Lego robot they'd built during the summer to clean up Legos (their mom had said, "How meta!"), and Willow showed off the computer program she'd written from scratch to chat with her friends over the Internet. Suddenly the committee was convinced.

Linden drew shapes in his head, thinking about the design. Elon was just plain awesome at building physical stuff, and Willow was going to write most of the computer code, so that left Linden with planning the structure and components. The plane needed to carry itself, a battery, a computer chip, a camera, and a transmitter to get the pictures back to the ground. He wondered whether Elon wanted to just take pictures to view later, or if he expected to see the video from the camera live while the drone was in the air.

He turned to whisper the question to Elon, but his seat was empty. He must have gone to the office after all. As Linden looked around, he noticed a lot of empty chairs, which was funny, because when they started school today, no one was absent.

CHAPTER THREE

On Wednesday, Willow's parents dropped them off at school. Elon and Linden ran outside to play while she met Atlanta in the cafeteria to hang out before school started. The ever-present food odors made her nauseous and glad she'd brought lunch from home.

"Let's get out of here," Atlanta said, obviously feeling the same way.

Willow nodded and they walked upstairs.

After being sick on Monday, Willow and Elon had to stay home on Tuesday. It was her first time back since leaving the classroom covered in vomit. Aside from Atlanta and Basil asking if she was okay, and a snide comment from Natalie, most of the rest of the class seemed to have forgotten about her throwing up on Monday. With so many kids that went home sick, apparently even projectile vomiting wasn't that re-markable.

"Twenty-three kids went home sick on Monday," Atlanta said. "The school nurse says it was stomach flu."

"I don't think so," Willow said. "It was what I ate." Even thinking about Monday's lunch made her queasy.

"Me, too," she said, but then the teacher came in and they had to cut their conversation short. They spent the morning learning kanji for foods and writing essays in Japanese about what their families ate at home. Then they had to read the essays out loud.

When Atlanta read "*Watashinokazoku wa yūshoku no tame ni inu o tabeta*," the class broke into laughter, because she said her family eats dogs.

"*Furankufuruto*," Akiyama Sensei corrected.

Later that day, after lunch, they went to Mrs. Dozen's classroom. Willow looked for the snake on entering, but Mr. E and his cage were gone. He'd been replaced by, of all things, an armadillo in a baby playpen.

The morning food theme continued, a conspiracy between their English and Japanese teachers.

Mrs. Dozen started class by showing them how to use a bread-maker. She mixed flour, yeast, salt and water, and then dumped the ingredients into the bread-maker.

After they each had a turn to watch the mixer in action, they took their seats.

"Where did the flour come from?" the teacher asked as the smell of warming dough wafted over the room.

She called on Maddie, a quiet girl sitting near the front.

"The grocery store," Maddie said.

"True," Mrs. Dozen said as she drew a box toward the right side of the board and wrote the word 'Store' inside the box. "Where did the grocery store get it? Any ideas?"

"A farm," Basil yelled out.

Mrs. Dozen walked to the other end of the long board, and made another box with the word "Farm" inside it. Then she looked at the white bag of flour with the yellow label. "Correct, but I'm pretty sure wheat doesn't grow in the form of a bag containing flour. Other thoughts?"

"A flour mill," Willow said, waving her hand in the air.

"Right, Willow," Mrs. Dozen said, as she added a box in the middle with the label "Mill". "What does the mill do?"

"Grinds the wheat seeds into flour."

"Very good, Willow. Now, how does the wheat get to the mill?"

Hands went up.

By the time they were done, a long diagram on the board stretched from the farm to Mrs. Dozen's kitchen, and in between sat trucks, mills, grain silos, and ware-houses.

Mrs. Dozen held up her hands for quiet. "How far do you think the food you eat has to travel from the place where it was grown or raised, to get to your plate?"

"A hundred miles," Basil said.

"Two hundred," Atlanta said.

"Five hundred miles," Willow said.

Mrs. Dozen picked up an orange off her desk and tossed it into the air while looking at it admiringly. "Where do oranges grow? How far away is that?"

Alice had her hand raised. "Florida. I saw orange farms when I visited."

Mrs. Dozen nodded. "They grow in warm places like Florida, California, and Texas." She picked up a banana. "Where does this come from?"

No hands went up.

The teacher waited for a minute. "Even warmer plac-es, tropical places. Mexico, Ecuador, Columbia, Panama. Do you think a truck drove this banana from Columbia to Portland? On average, the food you eat has traveled one thousand, five hundred miles to get to your plate. That means some has traveled less, but some has trav-eled more, much more. "

Now the diagram on the board got airplanes. And af-ter a discussion about how some fruits and vegetables have to be shipped before they're ready to eat (imagine mushy bananas bouncing around in a cargo hold), she also added ripening rooms at the distributor. They talked about trucks driving long distances across the United States, and how they needed air conditioning to keep the food cold, and how that added to the cost and environmental impact.

"Mrs. Dozen," Willow called out loud with her hand raised.

"Yes?"

"We raised money to get local, organic food in the cafeteria. I donated my own money. Where does that food come from?"

"Good question. The amount of money raised was about a hundred and twenty dollars per student. The purpose was to get local, organic food. There's no single definition of how far is still local, but often it's considered four hundred miles or less."

"So our lunch average is less than four hundred?" Willow asked.

"Not exactly. How many meals does a hundred and twenty dollars buy?"

The class shook their heads.

Basil raised his hand. "Lunch costs two dollars and twenty cents. So it's one hundred and twenty divided by two dollars and twenty cents."

Mrs. Dozen wrote the numbers on the board and did the math. It worked out to fifty-four lunches. But now she shook her head. "The cost of the ingredients is not the total cost of your lunch. Who makes your lunch?"

"Miss Berry!" Willow called out.

"Exactly. Miss Berry and other cafeteria staffed are employed by the school. But your lunch is also partly subsidized by the school, which means that you pay less than the full price. But it's still a good estimate, and if we don't have an exact number, an estimate is better than nothing."

Now she wrote more math on the board.

"The school year is more than fifty-four days long. It's about one hundred and seventy days. Which means that roughly one in three days is the local food you've paid for. So on about a third of days, the average distance your food travels is less than four hundred miles. All the rest comes from a lot farther away." She pointed to "1500" on the board.

Then the bread-maker dinged and the class rushed over.

Basil and Willow jockeyed for a place in line to get a slice. She wasn't exactly sure how long or how far the bread had to travel to get into her stomach, but it still tasted great.

CHAPTER FOUR

Elon and Linden sat together on the bus home. Elon drew a picture of an airplane with swept-back wings and a propeller in his notebook while Linden watched over his shoulder.

"We need to use a quadcopter, not a fixed-wing plane," Linden said. "A quadcopter is like a helicopter with four rotors, one at each corner." A football flew through the air, thrown from one of the forward rows, and Linden ducked just in time. It sailed overhead and went right out the window. "Oh, snap. Did you see—?"

"I know what a quadcopter is," Elon said, ignoring the football and other insanities of the school bus. "But a plane will be faster and have a longer flight time." He'd researched all kinds of autonomous drones before suggesting the project to his brother and sister.

"True, but you also want to put a camera on it. A quadcopter can hold steady to take better pictures."

Elon knew Linden was right, but he still had dreams of their drone swooping in like a fighter plane.

Linden must have seen the hesitation in his face. "Quadcopters can hover and pick up and drop off stuff. Some guys in England even built a copter that can carry a person!"

Elon jumped out of his seat. "Can we build one like that?"

"Sit down back there!" the bus driver called.

Linden shook his head. "No, but we can definitely carry the camera. We might be able to do a small grappling hook."

"Could we pick up someone's backpack?"

Linden shook his head no.

"Someone's lunch box?"

"No."

"A baseball?" Elon asked.

"Uh-uh."

Elon threw his hands up in the air. "Well then, exactly what can we carry?"

"Maybe a piece of paper."

"A piece of paper? What good is a piece of paper?"

Linden's head drooped. "Forget it."

Elon realized he'd hurt his brother's feelings. He needed Linden's help, though, so he had to be more diplomatic.

"Can you explain why?" Elon asked in his nicest voice.

Linden looked up. "We have to buy an ArduPilot, a frame, battery, engines, controller, and transmitter. We're borrowing the camera from dad. Between the three of us, we have barely enough money. If we want to carry more weight, we need bigger engines, which cost more money."

"How much more for the bigger engines?" Elon asked.

"Fifteen dollars."

"We can get that. We can wash mom and dad's cars. Twice." The going rate was four dollars per car.

"But if we have bigger engines," Linden said, "then we need a bigger battery and bigger motor controllers, and if we have those, then we need a bigger frame."

"How much does all of that cost?"

"A hundred dollars," Linden said. Just then two wrestling boys flew into their seat, landing in Linden's lap.

"Stay in your own seats!" the bus driver yelled.

The wrestling boys went back across the aisle.

Elon did the math in his head. They needed to have the project done in three weeks. He didn't want to wash mom and dad's cars twenty-five times, and besides, they probably wouldn't pay to have them washed more than once per day.

"OK, a piece of paper it is. We'll figure out something to do with that. Show me the design."

Linden flipped open his notebook and showed off his plans. "We'll use Willow's laptop to monitor the drone's camera in real-time. We can take photos or video."

"How fast can it go?" Elon asked. He had a vision of racing after cars to take pictures of their license plates.

"Twenty miles per hour. At least."

So not racing after cars. "Well, how far can it go?"

"It should be able to fly for fifteen to twenty minutes, but it depends on exactly how heavy it is."

Elon was deep in thought when he noticed Linden staring at him. "I'm trying to figure out something useful we can do," Elon explained. "The science fair judges are going to ask what we learned or what we can use the invention for."

"We can use it to take pictures of criminals," Linden said. "You know, we can match people with the wanted posters at the post office."

Elon nodded vigorously. "Sure, or we could pick up our homework at school when we're absent."

Willow was sitting four rows back, but she must have been able to hear their conversation, because she popped up and yelled, "Or we can use it to fly over a neighborhood and take pictures of all the animals to find lost dogs."

"Brilliant!" Elon yelled back, half standing.

"Sit down back there!" the bus driver roared.

Linden smiled and said quietly, "Willow loves animals. It's good she's excited."

"Exactly." They were both worried that Willow might back out of the project. It's going to take their combined savings and Willow was the only one that knew how to program computers.

CHAPTER FIVE

On Friday morning, Linden played wall ball with Kazuki and a group of boys in the schoolyard. He was just about to serve when another kid bumped into him, and then, without apologizing, kicked the wall ball halfway across the field. Linden's heart sank. Why did people do stuff like that? There were only a few minutes left to play before the bell rang.

By the time he got the ball, the bell rang for class. He stuffed the ball into his pack, then swung it onto his sweaty back and ran for the door. He found Elon just outside playing a videogame with another kid. He stopped to watch Elon hack and slash at zombies until a teacher yelled at them to go inside.

They bolted for their classroom, but stopped short midway through the school. Basil had set up shop in the main hallway by the front entrance.

"Hi Basil!" Linden yelled.

Basil was surrounded by piles of hair, Principal Winterson, Vice Principal Henry, and half the office staff. He must have started his science-fair hair-braiding project.

"I asked for permission to cut their hair," he argued.

"It's simply not okay to cut students' hair on school grounds," Principal Winterson said.

"Why?" Basil asked.

"First of all, it's dangerous. You shouldn't be using scissors like this and you need a license to cut hair."

"You only need a license to get paid for cutting hair," Basil said. "I'm not getting paid. And we use scissors every day in school."

Linden was impressed Basil had done his research.

"You're still not cutting hair on school grounds. You'll return that hair to the students you took it from."

Basil, Elon, and Linden all looked sideways at Mrs. Winterson. Return their cut hair? Basil appeared dumbfounded too.

"And then I'll want to discuss this with your parents."

Linden was dying to know what was going to happen,

but he and Elon were ushered to class by the school counselor.

In their classroom, Linden noticed a lot of girls with short, uneven hair. He didn't see any boys with haircuts, but then few boys had hair long enough to be worthwhile to the hair-braiding project.

In class, their teacher reviewed the bridge-research assignment. "You've all picked your bridges, and you should have started your research. You have one week left to turn in the first draft of your report, which should be two pages long. And remember, no using Wikipedia."

Linden groaned inside. Teachers were always saying they shouldn't use Wikipedia, but he loved, loved, loved everything about it. He raised his hand.

"Yes, Linden?"

"We should be allowed to use Wikipedia," he said. "Wikipedia is equally accurate *and* more comprehensive than traditional encyclopedias."

"Anyone can edit Wikipedia. It's simply not a credible resource."

Linden's felt his blood start to pound in his ears. He respected his teachers, but they weren't always right. "But it's been studied by dozens of researchers, and they've found it has high quality, even in specialized subjects. Even if someone puts incorrect information into Wikipedia, the editors usually spot and correct it within minutes."

The teacher tapped her foot. Linden couldn't tell if she was annoyed or amused.

She looked at the wall for moment, then turned back to the class. "Regardless of the accuracy of Wikipedia, if you all do your research using it, everyone's reports will look exactly the same. Each person researching the Fremont Bridge will read the same information, and I'll get back ten of the same reports. So no Wikipedia."

The teacher's point was good. But Linden knew some secrets about Wikipedia. Some of the best stuff was not in the main page for an article, it was hidden on the Talk page. That's where the people writing an article had discussions. And if two people disagreed about a subject, the history of their arguments was preserved forever on the talk page.

That wasn't the only secret, of course. The History link displayed every change ever made on a Wikipedia page, so visitors could know what had been deleted or added.

Linden had already started his research on the St. Johns Bridge last night. After he read the main article on Wikipedia, he discovered on the Talk page that there was a disagreement over whether the bridge should have an apostrophe in the name. Should it be written St. Johns or St. John's? It turned out the bridge was named after James John, also known as "Old Jimmy Johns" or "Saint Johns." Since Johns was his nickname, the name of the bridge shouldn't have an apostrophe in it. And yet the main article hadn't said anything about who the bridge was named after.

He'd also checked to see what had changed in the last year, figuring that it was an old bridge, so any change would reflect recent news. The main difference was a note that the St. Johns bridge had been used in a TV show filmed in Portland.

Wikipedia had all these cool secrets to uncover.

CHAPTER SIX

It was Saturday morning and Willow worked on the drone with Linden and Elon. Her brothers had gone to the hobby store yesterday with dad, and came home with what seemed like hundreds of parts that were now spread across the project table in the garage.

She'd brought her laptop into the garage, too, and was reading the documentation for ArduPilot, the auto-pilot computer and software that would fly their quadcopter. Even before her brothers finished building the hardware, she could test the software with a simulator. Right now Willow had bits of circuit boards plugged into each other, and she configured the ArduPilot software to explain what type of airplane they were building and which GPS they'd use. The GPS was a radio receiver that listened for satellites and could figure out exactly where in the world it was. They'd use it to let the plane find itself on a map. It was critical to allow the copter to fly itself around.

When the software was configured with the basics, she read instructions on how to set up the camera to take a photo every fifty feet. She daydreamed about having the copter fly back and forth in a pattern, taking photos automatically until she had a picture of every backyard in the neighborhood.

By lunchtime the boys had the frame of the copter assembled and they wanted to put the electronics in place. Willow reluctantly surrendered the circuit boards, and focused instead on connecting the transmitter to the software. The transmitter would let them take a picture or control the grappling hook from the ground, and fly the copter on manual control.

After a glance at the clock on her computer, Willow started to rush. She had to finish up, because Atlanta would be over soon, and they were going to the park to ride bikes. Suddenly the house phone rang, and her mom called Willow to get the phone in the kitchen.

"Hello?"

"Hi, Willow. This is Atlanta's mom. Atlanta can't meet you today. She has another stomachache."

Willow was silent as disappointment filled her, then

said weakly, "I hope she feels better. Thank you for letting me know."

She hung up, and remembered that Atlanta hadn't been feeling good yesterday afternoon, right after lunch. Atlanta had eaten hot lunch again, some sort of meat thing, which Willow had passed over in favor of a peanut butter and jelly sandwich.

On Monday, they'd eaten the same thing, and both of them got sick. Yesterday, Atlanta was hot lunch again and got sick again, but Willow's sandwich seemed fine. Maybe there wasn't a stomach flu going around. Maybe it really was the food. She grew suspicious something was wrong with their school lunches.

"What did you have for lunch this week?" Willow asked the boys on returning to the garage.

"The same thing as always," Linden said. "Spaghetti, bread, and rice."

Linden was a fan of plain white, tan or brown foods and always brought his own lunch except for Brunch for Lunch Day, because pancakes fit within his color palette.

"Did you ever feel sick this week?"

"Nope," Linden said.

"And you, Elon?"

"Umm..." He was surrounded by wires and small circuit boards and electric motors. "What?"

"What did you have for lunch this week?"

"I can't remember," he said.

This was a problem. It was just plain hard to remember what you ate several days ago. She'd read enough detective novels to know that good detectives kept meticulous notes. She'd need a chart of what people ate and whether they got sick or not.

"How's the auto-pilot coming?" Elon asked.

"Good." Willow got back to work and forgot about food for a while.

Before they knew it, their dad was calling them to come in. They stopped only with reluctance, because they were making good progress. They might get a flight in with another day of work.

Their mom reminded everyone to dress up because they were going to a fancy restaurant to entertain an out-of-town coworker. Willow changed into a black dress with tights and came out to see Linden and Elon in pants and button-down shirts. For boys, and especially her brothers, they looked pretty sharp. Just for the heck of it, she gave them both hugs before they got in the car.

The restaurant had candles on the table (a good sign) and it was quiet (potentially troubling since Linden and Elon frequently weren't), but after one glance from mom and dad, they decided to behave. The kids sat at one end of the table so the adults could talk.

Somehow Willow ended up sandwiched between the boys, and of course got kicked. In the legs. Like ten times. But the food was worth it. The adults raved over salad greens (were they rabbits?) and local fish. Willow ordered salmon and broccoli, Elon got gnocchi with truffle sauce, and Linden—somehow—managed to get plain spaghetti and butter, which wasn't even on the menu.

Willow speared one stalk of broccoli with her fork and stared at it before taking a bite. It was crisp, bright green, and tasted good. The menu made a big deal about how all the food was local and fresh. This was puzzling, because their school lunches were also supposed to be local and fresh, but didn't look or taste at all similar. What was going on?

CHAPTER SEVEN

Willow picked over her lunch on Monday. Unfortunately, she'd chosen hot lunch today, some kind of mystery meat. Why, oh why, hadn't she brought lunch from home? The school lunch tasted and smelled funny in addition to the odd gray color.

Atlanta bit into hers, then got a funny look on her face. She dug around with her fingers, and pulled out a small metal ball. "A BB!" she said.

Willow threw down her fork and pushed the plate away. "I'm done with this. My broccoli looks like it was sitting out on the counter all week. My apple is more bruises than not."

"I don't understand," Atlanta said. "Is this the food we donated extra money to get?"

Willow eyed her milk, suddenly suspicious, but it looked like the same milk they got every day.

Basil sat down next to them with his usual peanut butter and jelly sandwich. He slid the apple over to Willow.

She pushed it towards Atlanta, who pushed it back to Basil.

He ignored it.

"What's with the bandaids?" Willow asked. Nearly every finger on his hand had one or more bandages.

"Grrr. Arrgh."

"Articulate as usual. What gives?" she asked, turning to Atlanta.

"On Friday he got in trouble for cutting hair at school," Atlanta said.

"I still say there's no rule against cutting hair at school." Basil bit furiously into his sandwich.

"And on Saturday I was still sick," Atlanta said, "so Basil went to the high school track meet, and told the cheerleaders he was collecting hair to donate to charity—"

"Which we will!" he interrupted.

"And so he got all the hair we needed." Atlanta started to break down in giggles.

"What the what!" Basil said. "I've never braided hair before."

"On Sunday, he started braiding. I was still sick. How long did you braid for?"

"I braided hair, by myself, for ten hours. Ten hours!" He wiggled his hands at me. "These are blisters. Apparently I can rock-climb with no problem, but I can't braid hair."

Willow was fascinated. She couldn't imagine Basil working that hard on a school project. "How much rope do you have?"

"We don't have rope yet," Basil said. "We just have yarn."

Willow was puzzled. "Now you're making yarn?" she said. "Did you turn this into a crochet project?"

"No," Atlanta answered between bites of her mystery meat. "It takes several stages. Small bundles of hair have to be twisted together to make plies or singles. It's like thread or string. Then we take those singles and twisted them together to make three-ply rope."

"Yeah, it's really fun," Basil said, with a fake smile planted on his face. "You want to work on it with us?" He made puppy-eyes at Willow.

"No thanks, I'm good with our drone."

His face sagged and he turned to Atlanta. "You're going to help with the next part, right?"

"Of course," she said. "I don't want to be sick, you know."

But later that day, a bunch of kids, including Atlanta, asked to be excused to the office and didn't come back to class. By the end of the school day, the rumor was that thirty kids had gone home sick.

Willow called her that night and her dad picked up. "Is Atlanta home?" she asked.

"She's at the hospital with her mom," he said.

"Hospital?" Willow's stomach dropped and her heart beat faster.

"Yes, Willow. I don't know what's going on with this stomach flu she has, but every time we think she's better, she gets sick again."

Willow panicked. If Atlanta went to the hospital, it was serious. She didn't remember hanging up, but the next thing she knew, she was in her brothers' room, sitting on Elon's bed, crying.

"What's the matter?" Linden asked.

"It's the food."

Linden looked puzzled.

"The food at school. It's why kids keep getting sick, I'm sure of it."

Linden, who only ate spaghetti or rice from home, didn't know what Willow was talking about.

"Come on, Elon, you've seen it, right?"

Elon nodded. "The vegetables are soggy and the meat tastes funny."

"But not all the time," Willow said. "Some days it's normal, and some days it's not." She looked them both in the eyes. "I need your help. We have to solve this mystery."

Linden stared back at her. "Shouldn't we let adults handle this?"

"Adults are clueless. They're always looking at their phones, reading email, or going on Facebook. They don't pay attention."

"That's true," Elon said.

Willow remember the lesson in Mrs. Dozen's class, the way the food came from farms, was received by distributors in one area, who then shipped the food to distributors in other areas. Their cafeteria food could be coming from anywhere! "We need to talk to Miss Berry in the cafeteria, and find out where the food is coming from. We need to trace the food step by step back to its source."

"How are we going to do that?" Elon asked.

"I don't know, but we have to figure out a way. Otherwise kids might start to die."

CHAPTER EIGHT

Tuesday morning, they got to school early, shaking the water off their raincoats as they entered the cafeteria. Even in this rain, they passed Kazuki playing soccer outside.

"I want to play with Kazuki and Bobby!" Linden said.

"Yeah, me too," Elon said. He could just imagine Bobby doing a drop-kick the length of the schoolyard.

"We have to do this together," Willow said, her voice tight. "Besides, Bobby isn't—

"But why?" Elon interrupted. "You could talk to Miss Berry by yourself."

Willow shook her head.

Elon guessed she was nervous, and it was easier to do stuff that makes you nervous when you're with a friend. Well, Willow was helping them with the drone, so he'd help her with this. "No problem. We'll come with you."

They walked together into the kitchen. Normally they only came in for lunch. At this early hour, Miss Berry looked even busier than she did at lunchtime, rushing between unloading food, selling breakfast items, and re-loading lunch cards for parents.

They waited for a gap, then Willow called out, "Miss Berry."

Miss Berry rushed over from unloading buns. "Yes?"

Willow cleared her throat. "Where does our food come from?"

Miss Berry, already frantic, looked back towards the buns, and then toward the cash register. She didn't seem like she had much time, but she took a deep breath, and visibly slowed down a bit. "Do you mean how does it get here, or where is it grown?"

Willow looked at Elon to take over.

Elon swallowed deeply. "We want to know the whole thing," he said "Where is it grown? How did it get here?" He spontaneously pointed at a pile of hamburger patties. "Who made the meat into the hamburger?"

Miss Berry sighed. "I don't know, kids." She stopped and looked around the kitchen. "I probably have fifty different foods around here, from the breakfast items that are out now, the three different lunch choices for today, all the condiments. I don't know where it all comes from."

"What about the local foods we paid extra money for?" Linden asked.

"Oh, don't get me started about that program," Miss Berry said, turning to check out a kid getting cereal and a muffin for breakfast. "They said local and fresh. I haven't seen anything show up that's been local and fresh. More like wilted and old. Mondays and Fridays are the so-called local and fresh days. But it's garbage. I don't understand it."

"But where does it come from?" Willow asked again.

"I'm sorry," Miss Berry said, shaking her head. "I just don't know. Everything is dropped off twice a week. We get a delivery early Monday morning, and another one early Thursday morning. Bannon Foods is the company that delivers."

"They deliver everything?" Elon asked.

"Yes, they're a food distributor. They gather together everything, and deliver it to us."

"So they'll know where everything comes from?" Linden said.

"I suppose so," Miss Berry said. "Now I really gotta go, kids."

She rushed back to unload juice boxes, and they turned to each other.

"This is perfect," Willow said.

"How is it perfect?" Elon asked. "We didn't learn anything."

"We learned that everything comes from Bannon Foods," Willow said. "Now we can visit them and ask them where the food comes from."

"Why would they tell us?" Linden asked. "Why would they talk to a bunch of kids at all?"

Willow tapped her foot for the moment. "I got it! We'll tell them we're doing a report on the school food supply chain, and find out where everything comes from."

"Good idea, but what's all this 'we' business?" Elon said. "We need to work on the science-fair project. Can't this wait?"

"With people getting sick?" Willow said. "No way. This is important."

The bell rung for them to go to class. Screams almost drown out the pounding of hundreds of running students as everyone ran for class. None of the three made a move.

Elon looked down at his black and red sneakers. He didn't want to visit Bannon Foods, but he also didn't know how to explain this to Willow.

"We can do both," Linden said. "Let's do some research about them tonight on the Internet, and then visit them after school tomorrow."

"Right," Willow said. "Visiting them will just take one afternoon. We can work on the drone this weekend."

"Fine," Elon said, nervous about the distraction, and thinking about the wires he needed to solder to connect the motors. It was his first time soldering, and he needed to get it perfect. "But promise me we'll work on the drone too. We need a test flight on Sunday."

Linden and Willow nodded, and Willow gave him a hug. "We'll get it done. Besides, we have to beat Atlanta and Basil's hair-braiding project, right?"

Then they streamed along with the last of the people going to class.

CHAPTER NINE

That night they gathered around dad's big-screen computer. Willow took the mouse with Linden and Elon on either side. They found the Bannon Foods website to be a series of boring company web pages, pretty much less useful than even the most basic blog.

The home page showed a photo of smiling workers loading pineapples into a truck in front of palm trees. There wasn't a palm tree within a thousand miles of Portland.

"It's not even Bannon Foods," Willow said. "It's just a stock photo the company bought to look good."

"Click there," Linden said, pointing to the Products page. The page loaded, displaying a long list of meats, vegetables, and canned goods. Willow scrolled through several pages. Everything any kind of restaurant might want, from prepared foods to raw ingredients, was there.

Willow clicked on the Contact Us web page. The address was in Southeast Portland, just a couple of miles from their school.

"Google Maps," Linden said.

Willow nodded, cut and pasted the address into Google Maps, and they stared at it.

"We could walk there after school, then take the bus home," she mused. She clicked on street view, and they saw a photo of the building from the road. It was just a plain building behind a chain-link fence with a lot of trucks in the parking lot. "Looks harmless enough."

"Search Google again," Linden said.

Willow put Bannon Foods back into the search engine and a list of websites popped up.

"Add 'complaints' to the search term," Linden said.

Willow searched again, so that it looked like *"Bannon Foods" complaints*.

The top link was to a website called BBB.

"The Better Business Bureau," Linden said. "They keep track of businesses."

Linden, as usual, was a fount of arcane wisdom regarding everything on the Internet.

Visiting the site, they found that Bannon Foods had a C rating from the Better Business Bureau, with eight complaints listed, all from the last year. One of them looked like this:

"We've been using Bannon for more than ten years with no problems. But in the last two months, we received several shipments of vegetables, which when we unboxed were noticeably wilted with brown spots. The company denied that the food was shipped in that condition, and refused to offer a refund, despite the fact that we were unable to use the vegetables."

And another one:

"Received shipment of poor quality meats. Bannon Foods was very good for many years, but we will be switching to a different food distributor now."

"All these complaints are from this year," Elon said, pointing to the dates on the screen.

"Yeah. Well, are we up for visiting them after school tomorrow?"

"Let's do it," Linden said.

"We'll say we're doing a report for school," Willow said, "which is true enough, since it is what I'm studying."

"I'll bring my camera," Elon said, "and get pictures."

They checked out bus schedules, and found they could walk to Bannon Foods, spend an hour there, and still get home in time for dinner.

CHAPTER TEN

Linden shoved his backpack higher onto his shoulders, and ran over to Elon and Willow. They had a two-and-a-half mile walk ahead of them. Luckily, the light drizzle stopped after a few minutes. Linden jumped into a puddle.

"Stay clean!" Willow yelled. "We have to look presentable."

Linden and Elon looked sadly at each puddle they passed after that.

They strolled down Hawthorne Avenue, gazing in store windows at first, and then trudging slower and slower as the journey went on.

"Ice cream!" Elon called out, when they were about halfway there.

All three gazed into the window of the scoop shop.

"Chocolate," Elon mused. "With sprinkles."

"Vanilla," Linden said. "In a cone. Mmmm."

"Buy us ice cream, please, Willow." Elon looked up at her with puppy eyes.

Willow pulled out her wallet from her backpack and counted the money. "I think I have enough, if we each get a *small* cone."

"Thank you!" Linden hugged her.

They went inside and came out a few minutes later with ice cream and walked the rest of the way with renewed energy and happy smiles.

Forty minutes after school ended, they caught the first glimpses of the Willamette River between buildings. Shortly afterwards, they came to a big empty lot, with an unused warehouse.

"Is this it?" Linden asked, checking the address.

"No," Willow said. "It's the next one." She pointed farther down the block. From a slight rise they could see a giant blue building like a long barn, with a dozen trucks backed up to it at one side. Connected to one end was a much smaller building, also blue. While they watched, they saw a few people enter the smaller building. A parking lot held more small trucks with the Bannon name on the side, and a bunch of cars. The whole area was wrapped in a barbed-wire topped fence.

They glanced at each other.

"Notebook?" Willow asked.

"Check," Linden said.

"Camera?" Willow asked.

"Check," Elon said, taking it out of his backpack, and holding it tight in both hands.

"Well, I've got the questions, so let's go."

Inside the yard, a small black-and-white sign above one doorway declared it to be the "Office", so they headed there.

Pulling open the door, they stepped into adult land: white walls, brown desks, and paper. Paper everywhere. Piles of receipts, folders, food brochures. Their mom and dad complained that they used too much paper, but it wasn't even a hundredth of what was here.

A man looked up from a desk, appearing surprised to see kids. He checked behind them, like he was expecting someone else, probably a grownup. When no one else appeared, his gaze settled back on them.

As a group, they shuffled closer. After heated discussion and seven rounds of rock, paper, scissors, they'd agreed Linden would introduce everyone, and then Willow would take over the questioning.

"Hello?" the grownup asked, his mustache wiggling.

Linden swallowed deep and blurted out as quickly: "Hi, I'm Linden, and this is Willow and Elon. We're doing a school report on the food supply chain, and we found out you deliver the food for our school. We'd like to find out where it comes from." He managed to deliver this without taking a breath, and then held out his hand for a handshake. Apparently, when you did this, grownups had to respond with their name.

The grownup smiled. "How nice," he said, with a placating smile, as he reached out to shake Linden's hand. "I'm Brett. I have some brochures about what we do."

Linden reached out to take the brochures as all data was useful. But they'd expected the grownups would try to brush them off without really answering any questions and planned ahead.

"Thank you, Brett," Elon said. "But our teacher says we have to do our research in the form of an interview. Is there someone we can talk to? We just have a few questions."

Brett looked back to his desk. For some reason adults always wanted to get back to their paperwork and computers. "Why don't I see if our company president is available?"

Brett stood and disappeared through a doorway.

Elon pointed to the back wall of the office. A line of three black-and-white photographs showed Edward Bannon, Frank Bannon, and Tom Bannon from left to right. It looks like Edward Bannon founded the company in 1959, and ran the business for more than thirty years, until he turned it over to Frank in 1995. Frank ran the business until last year, and that left Tom.

The door opened, and Brett came through followed by Tom Bannon. Brett went back to his desk without another word, seeming glad to have handed them off to someone else. He got back into his paperwork without a second glance.

Tom had sandy hair, a friendly smile, and though he was an adult, he looked pretty young. Younger than their parents at least. "Hello kids," he said, approaching with his hand out. "I'm Tom Bannon."

They shook hands with him, one after another.

"Brett said you want to know more about our company."

"Yes, we're learning at Mt. Hood Elementary about food supply chains," Willow said, "and we'd like to interview you."

"How about we start with a little tour, and then you can ask me questions in my office?"

Tom was nice and helpful, and Linden instantly liked him.

"That would be great," Elon said.

"Well, I'm Tom. My grandfather, Edward, started this company." He gestured up toward the photographs they'd already discovered. "He turned it over to my father, Frank, who in turn gave the company to me when he passed away last year."

"I'm sorry, Mr. Bannon," Willow said.

Tom looked at the photograph of his father, distracted, then turned back to the kids. "That's all right. It was unexpected. I always knew he wanted me to take over the family business, but I didn't think it would be for a long time." He shook his head, then pointed at the room they were in. "This is the main office. It's where we take orders from restaurants, and place orders with suppliers."

"Do you just order what the restaurants want?" Linden asked.

"No, it doesn't work like that most of the time. Restaurants want their food for that week, but suppliers can take weeks to get food to us. So we have to guess what restaurants will want ahead of time, and order it. Some stuff is pretty routine. Mt. Hood Elementary is going to want three hundred hamburgers every Tuesday, and so that's easy. But a restaurant might say they want whatever fish is fresh as long as it's salmon, halibut or tuna. Some restaurants pay extra because they want what's local and fresh, and so they'll take whatever is in season right around here. We're a little unusual in that we service both institutional customers and premium restaurants."

They stared at him blankly.

"Sorry," Mr. Bannon said. "Institutional customers are school cafeterias, hospitals, and workplaces. They usually want a lot of the same food, pretty inexpensively.

Whereas a nice restaurant wants the best food they can get, even if that changes from week to week."

"Our school gets both," Elon said. "We get fresh, local foods on Monday and Friday, and the, uh, cheap food on the other days."

"So you do," Mr. Bannon said. "I forgot about that. I think it's the first time we've ever done that with a public school. Well, do you want to see the warehouse where we keep the food?"

"Yes, please," Linden said.

Mr. Bannon led them through a door into an immense warehouse. From here they saw a dozen enormous garage doors, half of which had trucks backed up to them. Inside the warehouse, small forklifts moved pallets of food, while other trucks were unloaded by hand.

They followed Mr. Bannon deeper into the warehouse.

"These are the dry goods," Mr. Bannon explained, pointing to immense shelves on their right. "This is where we have non-perishable goods that don't require refrigeration. That's stuff like flour, sugar, and oil, as well as spices and seasonings. We also have prepared food like crackers."

"Those are the biggest shelves I've ever seen," Willow said.

"They're called pallet racks," Mr. Bannon said, chuckling. "Each pallet is about four feet by four feet, and our racks go three levels up. The top level is twelve feet high, and can take a four foot tall pallet, which makes the very top..."

"Sixteen feet," Linden finished. He loved crackers, of any kind, and he stared at the largest container of saltine crackers he'd ever seen. It must have been four feet wide and four feet tall. "Who needs that many crackers?" he blurted out.

Mr. Bannon laughed. "Hopefully nobody. That's a full pallet of crackers, and we'll need to break that down into smaller boxes to send out to restaurants. It's in such a big container because it's easier to move with the fork-lift that way."

They trailed Mr. Bannon toward the trucks, but he suddenly turned them left, bringing them to a huge metal structure in the center of the warehouse. The whole place was way bigger than a soccer field, and the middle was taken up by a house-sized shiny white building.

"This is the part I always loved visiting as a kid," Mr. Bannon said. "It's our refrigerator. If you want to go inside, you have to put on a jacket." He led them to a row of winter parkers with furry hoods.

They each put one on. Linden laughed as Elon pulled the hood over his own head and disappeared inside the adult-sized parka. Then Mr. Bannon opened a small door, and they walked into the refrigerator. It was another warehouse, just on a smaller scale, and it was

COLD. Like winter-time cold. Clouds of frosty air circulated around them as they walked.

"This is where we keep produce that needs refrigeration, like vegetables, milk, eggs, and fresh meat. We have a separate freezer just for frozen foods like hamburgers and meats, but it's too cold to take you kids in there."

They stared in awe. The section just for eggs had to be ten feet long and equally tall. There must have been to be an entire truckload of eggs. Thousands of eggs, millions of eggs.

Linden hated eggs, and all he could think was *yuck!* but he didn't want to make Mr. Bannon feel bad, so he didn't say anything out loud.

By the time they got out of the refrigerator, Linden's fingers were frozen, and everyone's cheeks were red. They laughed with Mr. Bannon as they stamped their feet to get warm.

"That's fun, isn't it?" he said, with a big smile.

"It is," Willow said.

"Let's go see where they unload the trucks, next." Mr. Bannon hung up his parka and walked toward the door.

They rushed to follow, and Elon ran across the warehouse floor ahead of Mr. Bannon.

A loud beeping noise sounded from somewhere, and suddenly a forklift came around a corner, right toward Elon.

The forklift driver hit his horn. The loud blaring startled Elon, whose eyes went big as he dove toward a pallet of rice. The forklift swerved, nearly dropping its load of boxes, and narrowly missed Elon.

Suddenly an older man in a hardhat ran toward them, yelling.

"What the—" he yelled, then he saw Mr. Bannon. He pointed at the kids. "What the heck are they doing here, Tom?" He gestured all around the giant warehouse. "We're trying to work."

"Sorry, Jack, I'm just giving them a tour."

"Well, they could have gotten killed. The forklift would have crushed that kid." He punctuated each statement with a finger jab toward Mr. Bannon.

The adults kept arguing, Jack's arms moving wildly as he spoke, but they never stopped to check on Elon. Willow ran over to where Elon sat on a pile of rice bags. "Are you okay?"

Elon looked up, his eyes red like he wanted to cry, but he nodded and grabbed Willow's hand.

Mr. Bannon came over to them. "I'm sorry about that. It's my fault. I should have let Mr. Hutchins know we'd be back here." He glanced over to Jack Hutchins, but the older man just shook his head and walked away.

"Are you hurt?" Mr. Bannon asked Elon.

"I'm fine."

"Why don't we go back to my office."

They all nodded, subdued now, and stuck close to him.

When they got into Mr. Bannon's office, he pulled up an extra chair, so there was room for each of them to sit in front of his desk.

Mr. Bannon took his own seat. "Mr. Hutchins is our foreman and runs the warehouse. He's been with us since I was your age. Again, I'm really sorry about that forklift."

"It's okay," Elon said.

"Mr. Bannon," Willow started, "can you tell us where the food comes from for our school? Exactly which farms?"

"Mt. Hood Elementary orders a lot of food," he said. "It's not a short list. Let's look at a few things." He turned to his computer, then swiveled the monitor so they could see it too.

"Here's one week's delivery." He scrolled down through several pages, then went back up to the top. "Here's the first item. Three hundred pre-made hamburgers. They came from Beaverton Meat Processing. They do all the burgers for Portland schools. But I don't know where they get their meat from. Second item is two hundred pounds of pre-cut broccoli. We source that from Smith & Jones, a big food distributor in California. All of the vegetables come from them."

"All of the vegetables?" Willow asked, thinking of the wilted broccoli she'd tried to eat the other day.

"Anything in season, in the United States, yes. It's almost all grown in California."

"But what about the local foods?" Willow said. "I thought that's supposed to come from within four hundred miles."

"I forgot about that." He scrolled farther down in the list. "Yes, here we go. We've got another hundred pounds of fresh, uncut broccoli, for Monday delivery. That comes from Cascadian Falls, which is about fifty miles away. Good stuff, too. We use Cascadian Falls for local restaurants, too."

Linden suddenly felt inspired. Willow had mentioned the broccoli before. "Do you have any broccoli we can try? Can we see the difference?"

Mr. Bannon looked in the direction of the warehouse. "I don't think I should bring you back there again. But if you wait here, I'll get some."

He left, and they fidgeted in their chairs.

"Good idea," Willow said.

Linden smiled.

A few minutes later Mr. Bannon came back holding a head of broccoli in each hand.

"Here we go." He put each one down on the desk. "This one, on the left, is from Cascadian Falls. You can see the dark green color. It's a little smaller, but that's because it isn't watered so intensely. But it has a good, strong smell of broccoli, and a nice flavor."

Mr. Bannon's enthusiasm came through as he discussed the food. "On the right side we have the one from

Smith & Jones. It's a little bigger, a little paler, but still nice. You can see it's got a little bit of wiggle in it from the drive up by truck."

Willow picked up each one, smelled it and touched it, and then passed it on to the boys.

"I need to go in a few minutes," Mr. Bannon said. "I've got a phone call with one of our customers. I hope this was helpful."

"Yes, thank you," Willow said. "Is there any chance we could get a printout of the suppliers? Then we could draw them on a map."

Mr. Bannon thought for a minute. "Sure." He scribbled on a sticky note. "Bring this to Brett, and he'll print it out for you."

"Thanks a lot," Elon said.

Mr. Bannon shook hands with each of them, and then they left.

In the outer office, Brett looked at the sticky note and sighed, then a few minutes later handed them a thick printout stapled together.

As soon as they got outside, Willow blurted out, "That broccoli was nothing like what was served at school! The stuff at school was soggy and brown. There's something weird going on!"

"But what?" Linden asked.

"Maybe someone is stealing the broccoli," Elon said.

"Why would anyone steal broccoli?" Linden asked.

"That's crazy. I could understand maybe if someone stole ice cream, or cookies. It would be wrong, but at least there's be a reason for it. Besides, the broccoli isn't missing. It's just bad when it gets to school."

"I don't know," Willow said. "Maybe there's a broken refrigerator somewhere. Whatever it is, we're going to figure it out."

CHAPTER ELEVEN

On the way home, they took the streetcar to the #6 bus. Willow boarded deep in thought. "What did you guys notice there?"

"Mr. Bannon was nice," Linden said.

"I nearly died," Elon groaned.

"None of the food was rotten," Linden said, "even though you were sure it was going to be."

"Maybe they hid it because we were coming," Willow said.

"Nobody knew we were coming," Elon said. "They couldn't have hidden anything."

Linden pulled out a slice of toast and started eating.

"They could have hidden it while we were in that office with Brett."

"Where the heck did you get toast?" Willow asked.

"Bobby made it."

"Bobby is not—" Willow was cut off by a honking horn. She shrugged. "I think Elon's right, they couldn't have hidden anything. There wasn't time. But somehow that disgusting food is ending up in the school kitchen. Let's get to school early on Monday morning, really early, and watch them unload the food truck."

Elon shook his head. "No way, Jose. We already have to get up at six a.m. to be there by eight. I am not getting up any earlier."

"It's just one day. I promise to work on the drone all weekend."

"Promise?"

"Pinky swear."

"Starting as soon as we get home?"

"Yes, I will."

Elon held her to her promise. Once they arrived home, Willow barely had time to go to the bathroom before Elon was checking on her. She brought her laptop into the garage.

Linden and Elon had the quadcopter on the center workbench, arguing quietly over the motor attachments.

"Zip ties are what everyone uses," Linden argued.

"It's going to be ugly," Elon said. "I don't want random plastic clogging up our design."

"They're strong and lightweight," Linden countered. "That's why they're so popular."

Elon shook his head. "I need to it be beautiful, Linden. Grandpa didn't fix the dining-room table by screwing a sheet of plywood over the top, did he? No, he took the whole thing apart, planed it, glued it, finished it."

Willow smiled. Elon had a touch of the artist in him when it came to building. Willow couldn't help but get involved.

"What do you want to do?" Willow asked.

"The electric motor is round, and it's got a hole in the side of it. The aluminum strut it attaches to has two holes in it."

"For the zip tie to pass through," Linden interrupted.

"If I had a round plastic mount of just the right size," Elon said, ignoring Linden, "with two screw holes on the side, we could use a twenty millimeter screw to hold both the mount and motor, and then stabilize it with a second screw."

"You want to make it on dad's 3D printer?"

"Yeah, can you call him and ask him to bring it home from work?"

Willow called their dad, who said he'd bring the printer home. She checked thingiverse, the website for 3D printed parts, to see if she could find what Elon wanted.

She found eight hundred and seven motor mounts, including a few that were almost perfect. In the end, she downloaded a design, changed the position of the screw holes, and by the time their dad was home, had the print files ready to go.

They all gathered around the Makerbot as she printed the first mount. The fan spun up as the printhead heated to melt the plastic and soon the printer lurched into motion with a cacophony of noises as the printhead sped around the platform laying down plastic. Fifteen minutes later, the plastic part was done.

"Ow," Elon said, grabbing the still hot part off the platform. He trimmed the extra plastic off with a knife, and then fitted the motor mount in. The motor slid in easily. Too easily.

Willow's heart sank a little. The 3D printer was magical, but getting things exactly right was the hard part of the magic. She adjusted the inner diameter, and launched the second print. This time the motor mount was snug as it should be.

"Perfect!" Elon announced. "Make five more, please, so we can have spares."

Willow grumbled at Elon's bossiness, but set up the MakerBot for five more, which printed while they ate dinner.

CHAPTER TWELVE

"Put it over there," Elon said.

His father left the heavy tray of tools in the grass and retreated to the car to read a book. He'd offered to help, but Elon was sure they could do it themselves.

Elon and Linden carried the quadcopter over. The finished flying device looked like a giant X from the top, with a ten inch diameter silver propeller in each corner at the end of a long metal arm. Squat in the middle sat the electronics and battery pack, every wire carefully routed inside the aluminum metal frame. Each propeller sat on top of its own copper-colored motor, the motor being housed in the turquoise mounting brackets

Willow had printed last night.

Four plastic legs extended down, and Elon and Linden carefully rested the copter in the grass on these legs.

Willow brought her laptop computer, the radio controller, and extra batteries in an old green milk crate.

Elon felt a little vibration in his legs and arms, a bit of nervousness and lot of excitement. For this first flight, they just wanted to see it take off. They'd control it with the radio, and if it flew okay, then they'd do a short test with the autopilot in hover mode.

"Everyone ready?" Elon asked. He got nods in return. "Radio?"

"On," said Willow.

"Battery?

"Fully charged," said Linden.

He looked over at Willow. He really wanted to be the one to fly it first. The whole project had been his idea.

Willow looked back at him, and handed over the transmitter.

"Thank you," he said in a small voice.

Willow just smiled in return.

Elon checked the throttle stick to make sure it was fully down. "Turn it on."

Linden leaned down, flipped the switch and backed away.

Elon pushed up on the throttle and nothing happened. He flipped the throttle up and down twice more, still with no effect. The power light on the transmitter was on. Strange.

"Is the copter on?" he asked. "Nothing is happening."

Linden looked closely. "Yup. I can see light on the receiver. It's got power."

Elon sighed. "Let's shut it down and check the connections."

Twenty minutes later they'd worked through the battery connections, receiver connections, the electronic speed control wires, receiver antenna, and motor cables.

At thirty minutes their dad came over, but they shooed him away.

At forty minutes, Elon was checking the radio transmitter. The radio station of the transmitter and receiver had to match. "What frequency is it set for?" he asked.

"They should find each other on C band," Linden said.

"Well, this is set for D band," Elon said. He flipped a switch.

"Bobby must have done it," Linden said. "Right, Bobby?"

Willow yelled, "Bobby IS NOT—"

But the blades on the drone began to spin, a high-pitched mini-roar that drowned out Willow's words, and the copter lifted off the grass!

"Yes!" Linden shouted, and then he and Willow high-fived.

Elon couldn't believe it—the quadcopter was actually flying! And he was flying it.

They flew a dozen more times that day. Linden and Willow each wanted turns, just taking off, hovering, and landing again.

On Elon's next turn, he pushed forward, and the copter flew away. He gently pushed left, and the quad-copter began making a long, slow curve. He wanted to shout and jump up and down, but he couldn't let go of the controller, not for an instant.

Of course, then Linden and Willow wanted to fly it in circles, too.

Their dad came back from the car to watch.

All this was fun, but it was just testing the motors, frames, and receiver. What they really wanted was to test the autopilot.

They powered down one last time. Now Elon flipped the switch on the ArduPilot board. He looked to Willow, who had her laptop powered up.

"Got it," she said, when the laptop had connected with the brains of the autonomous drone, so she could trigger and monitor the autopilot.

Elon turned on the power to the rotors and backed away. Now it was Willow's turn to control the drone by telling the autopilot what to do.

"Turning on autostabilization and setting it for an al-titude of three feet." It was a simple test, but it would let them know if the autopilot software on the drone was capable of controlling the little quadcopter by itself. She input the data, then clicked enter.

The drone came to life, propellers whirling into a blur, then lifted off the ground. It rose three feet into the air, and hovered motionless.

They all whooped, then gathered around it. Using the ground-facing ultra-sonic range finder, the drone could see exactly how far it was from the ground. At least when it was below fifteen feet. Above that, it needed to use the GPS, which wasn't nearly as accurate. But the ultra-sonic range finder was good for within a few inches. And they could see it doing that now: maintaining a nearly perfect thirty-six inches off the ground, only gently moving and then coming back when there was a breeze.

"We have to name it," Willow said. It felt like the right thing to do. Years ago they had named their dad's remote-control car Chitty Chitty Bang Bang, after the car from the movie.

"The Buzzing Hornet," Linden said. "It sounds like one."

"The Flying Wonder," Willow suggested.

"It's got silver propellers," Elon said, "and it roars as it flies. Let's call it the Silver Dragon."

CHAPTER THIRTEEN

The alarm went off early Monday morning, too early. Willow's head swam as she shut off the buzzer. Why was it five a.m.? She sat on the edge of her bed, befuddled. Oh, right! It was Monday morning. They had to get to school early to watch the unloading of the supply truck.

It was still pitch-black out. Willow jumped out of bed, and fell with a thud onto the floor. Her feet were still tangled up in her blankets.

She distantly heard her parents calling to see if she was all right.

"I'm fine," she yelled back, then slowly and more gracefully got back to her feet. She went to her brothers room, and woke them up. At least, she tried to. They slept like logs. She had to shake Linden back and forth a dozen times before he even started to respond. Finally, she had to pull all the covers off them.

"Wake up!" she said in an urgent whisper. "We have to get to school early for the truck."

"It's too early," Linden said, and pulled his pillow over his head.

"Come on, if we don't solve this mystery, people will get sick. People could die. Atlanta could die."

Finally they sat upright, and walked like groaning zombies into the bathroom.

She dashed back into her own bedroom, threw on her clothes, and ran downstairs.

She poured cereal and milk for everyone. When Linden and Elon came down, they all ate in silence.

"Ten minutes till the bus. I'll go tell mom and dad we want to take the bus on our own."

Everyone dashed up from their seats, cleared their places, and grabbed their backpacks. Willow ran upstairs and came back down a minute later.

"Ready?" Willow asked as they assembled by the door.

"What did mom and dad say?" Elon asked.

"I think they seemed happy to sleep in. They said to be careful and take the right bus."

On the way to the bus stop, Linden turned to Willow.

"You owe us chocolate chip cookies for getting up this early."

"I'll bake a double batch when we get home."

When they arrived at school, the Bannon Foods truck was just backing up to the loading area. They ran the last half block and made it to the back of the truck before the driver got out.

"What are we looking for again?" asked Linden.

"This is the Monday delivery," Willow said. "So it'll have the local foods on it. We're checking to see if the food is good or bad."

"Why?" asked Elon.

"If the food is good, then it means that the problem is in our cafeteria. Probably Miss Berry is in on it. If the food is bad, then it means Miss Berry is innocent, and the problem is at Bannon Foods or before."

"Then we have to hide somewhere," Elon said. "We can't hang around here and have the driver see us. What if he's in on it?"

"Good point," Willow said. She glanced around. "Elon, you stay by the bicycle rack, pretend you're locking up your bicycle, and watch him unload. Linden, you go to the front counter and distract Miss Berry. I'll sneak into the kitchen, hide in a closet and watch them unload."

"I'll have Bobby come with me!" Linden said.

"Bobby's not..." Willow trailed off as Linden had already turned the corner.

Linden ran around the school at top speed to the cafeteria entrance. It was so early he was the second kid in the school. He entered the kitchen from the front entrance, picked up a cinnamon breakfast bar, glanced at the ingredient list, and then called Miss Berry over.

"I'm allergic to allow-allow nuts, Miss Berry. Does this have any in it?"

Miss Berry grabbed the bar away. "Oh dear. I've never heard of an allow-allow nut. Let me check." She read through the list of ingredients. "No, it seems fine."

Linden saw Willow enter the kitchen from the maintenance door, hunting for a hiding spot. He needed to delay longer.

"Does it have pickleberries? That's a wild relative to the strawberry, and I'm not supposed to have that either."

"A pickleberry? I've never heard of it." Miss Berry peered closely at him. "You've never mentioned food allergies before."

"That's because I only eat brunch for lunch, and I know what's in the pancakes."

Miss Berry nodded as though that made sense, and read through the ingredients. "No pickleberries." She handed it back.

Willow was just crawling under a counter with a good view of the entrance, but the spot was so small it was taking a long time for her to squash herself in.

"And the wheat. Do you know if it's GMO? My mom says not to eat genetically modified foods."

Miss Berry grabbed the bar back from him, and gripped it a little tightly. Cream cheese oozed out of the ends. He hated cream cheese. She finished looking at the ingredients. "It doesn't say whether the wheat is GMO or not."

Willow was fully under the counter, and he could quit stalling. "Oh, that probably means it is. I'd better not get it. Thanks for your help, Miss Berry!"

On the other side of the kitchen, Willow wedged tightly under the counter. The space was so small she had to fold up into a square, like that time when a big package had been delivered to their house, and they all took turns folding up to fit into the cardboard box. But she had an excellent view of the floor, and unless someone looked directly under the counter, they wouldn't spot her.

The hand truck rolled into view, and Willow realized her first mistake. She couldn't see the driver's face, because the counter blocked her view.

"How are you, Ada?" the driver called.

"Just fine? And you?" Miss Berry replied.

Willow had no idea Miss Berry's first name was Ada. She tried to reach for something to write this down, but she couldn't move her arms she was so squished in.

The hand truck had three cardboard boxes covered in frost.

"Hamburgers, hamburgers, and more hamburgers," the driver said.

Willow saw Miss Berry's legs walk over to a giant stainless steel freezer and open the door. The driver carried two boxes and Miss Berry one. The driver disappeared for a few minutes, until he came back with three more boxes. "Breakfast bars, chicken patties. Stir-fry beef."

The boxes were put into a different refrigerator and the driver went away. He came back a few minutes later with black plastic crates, with greens sticking out. "Two crates local broccoli, one crate local Brussels sprouts."

Willow was ten feet away, but as the hand truck went by, she could smell a slight off odor.

"Oh, not again," Miss Berry called. "Come on, look at this broccoli. This isn't fresh!"

"Sorry, Ada. I just drive the truck."

"But every week it comes in like this. The kids paid extra money for this stuff."

The driver walked over to Miss Berry's side.

"It does look a little funny."

Willow breathed a quiet sigh of relief. Miss Berry was in the clear. The food was coming into the school in this rotten state, so it definitely wasn't the fault of Miss Berry or the school kitchen.

This meant they'd have to pay another visit to Bannon Foods.

CHAPTER FOURTEEN

Elon's teacher passed around a paper handout.

"I'd like you all to read this poem composed by Bobby for last week's homework assignment."

There was a slight chuckle from the class, and Elon and Linden smiled at each other. They'd turned in the poem for Bobby.

"Now, looking at Bobby's work, I want to ask you, what's makes it a poem?"

Linden's hand shot up to answer "rhyming," but just then there was a knock at the door. It was Mr. Henry, the vice principal. "Elon, Linden, can I talk to you?"

Oh, snap. Linden and Elon glanced at each other and went to the door.

Mr. Henry closed the door, and they stood in the hallway looking at each other.

"Did Willow come to school today?"

Linden's eyes went big. It was fifteen minutes since school had started, and he hadn't seen Willow since she'd hidden under the kitchen counter. He glanced over at Elon, but Elon just shrugged his shoulders slightly.

"Yes, Mr. Henry," Elon said. "But she stopped to get some food."

"Maybe she's still in the cafeteria!" Linden said. "We'll go get her!"

Linden and Elon raced off, knowing their only chance was to get to the cafeteria before Mr. Henry and extract Willow from the kitchen. Miss Berry must still be there and would need distracting again.

"Come back," Mr. Henry called, but Linden and Elon put on extra speed, and ran so fast the posters in the hallway rattled with their passing.

They peeled into the cafeteria so hard their sneakers squeaked and skidded on the wax floor. They ran for the kitchen. They probably had less than a minute before Mr. Henry caught up.

"We're gonna be in so much trouble," Linden gasped.

"We're saving lives," Elon said as they slammed up against the kitchen doorway with an oof.

Miss Berry was nowhere to be seen.

"Willow?" Elon called.

"Help, I'm stuck under here. Hurry before Miss Berry comes back!"

They ran into the kitchen, found Willow still under the counter.

"I can't move. The space is too tight. Yank me out!"

They each grabbed an arm and pulled. After a moment, Willow dislodged, and they all flew backwards.

Willow stood on shaky legs.

"We gotta hurry, Mr. Henry is looking for you," Linden said. "We have to get back to class."

They ran out, Willow hobbling along behind on pins-and-needles feet. They met Mr. Henry in the hallway outside the cafeteria.

"What's going on?" Mr. Henry said.

"We found Willow," Elon said. "Just like we said we would. You're welcome, Mr. Henry." He moved to walk back to class.

"Not so fast. " Mr. Henry said. "Where were you?" he asked Willow.

Willow stared up at Mr. Henry. She didn't really want to say what she was doing until she had solid evidence so people would believe her. But lying to Mr. Henry would be wrong. "I was in the kitchen. Mr. Henry, kids keep getting sick. I think it's the school lunches that are making kids sick. I wanted to inspect the food."

Mr. Henry stared at Willow for a second. "You're friends with Atlanta, aren't you?"

Willow nodded.

"Is this about her going to the hospital?"

"Yes."

Mr. Henry turned to Linden and Elon. "You can go. I'll talk to your sister."

CHAPTER FIFTEEN

Willow sank gratefully into a seat at the lunch table next to Atlanta, and hugged her

"Where's my hug?" Basil asked.

Willow turned to Atlanta. "You're okay."

"Of course I'm okay. Why wouldn't I be?"

"You weren't available this weekend, again."

Atlanta said something under her breath, too quiet for Willow to hear.

"She was sick," Basil said. "Couldn't help with the science-fair project, again."

Willow couldn't help but notice the bitterness in Basil's voice. It didn't sound like kidding around anymore.

"Are you two okay?" Willow asked.

"I don't want to do this project by myself," Basil said, loud enough that people looked at them.

"And it was my idea, so of course I want to work on it," Atlanta said through clenched teeth. "How about you spend all weekend in bed, and I'll braid hair? *Excuse me.*" Atlanta ran off to the bathroom.

Willow went with her.

"You're not really okay," Willow said.

Atlanta's eyes were red like she wanted to cry. "No, I'm tired of being sick. But tell me about this morning. I heard you went to the counselor's office."

"Yeah, Mr. Henry found out I was hiding in the cafeteria kitchen. I was watching the food delivery, to find out whether the food arrived bad, or got that way afterwards."

"And?"

"The food is bad when it gets here. So the problem is with Bannon Foods."

"No, no," Atlanta said. "What happened with Vice Principal Henry?"

"Oh. He and the counselor and I got together, and they made me talk about my feelings"—Willow rolled her eyes— "and then they concluded I was just worried about you, and took pity on me, and I didn't get in any more trouble."

"Did they believe you about the food?"

"No," Willow said, "they ignored that part."

"It's like my dad says."

"What?"

"Just because you're paranoid," Atlanta said, "doesn't mean people aren't out to get you."

"What does that even mean?" Willow asked.

"I think it means that you can be scared of something and something might be real, or it might not, but just because you're scared doesn't tell you whether it's actually risky," said Atlanta. Then she changed the subject. "Why do your parents let you take the bus all over town?"

"My dad grew up in New York City," Willow said, "and kids there always took the buses and subways by themselves."

"Aren't you afraid? What if you get lost?"

"I'd stop someone and ask them for help."

"Aren't you afraid—"

"No," Willow said. "Google 'free range kids'. It's about this nine-year-old kid who wanted to see if he could get home on his own if his mom dropped him off in a strange part of town."

"What happened?"

"He got home. I think it's like you said. People get scared of kids going around by themselves, but it's safer than most people think."

On the way out of the bathroom, they ran into Elon and Linden. Willow explained what happened after they'd gotten her out of the kitchen.

"You know what this means?" Willow asked. "We're going to have to get up way earlier. We have to get to Bannon Foods to see who loads the truck, and whether the food is good or bad then."

"Why?" asked Atlanta at the same time that Elon and Linden said "No way!"

"Because if good food goes onto the truck," Willow said, "and bad food comes off, then we know it's the truck driver swapping out the food before he gets here. He could be selling the local food we've paid for, and then getting cheap food somewhere else, and keeping the profits."

"We already got up at five this morning!" Elon said. "We're not getting up earlier."

"How else are we going to learn if it's the driver?"

"Oh, man," Elon said. "We have to do it, don't we?"

"If we want to solve this mystery, we do."

CHAPTER SIXTEEN

Linden and Bobby crested the sand dune and found a pirate ship washed up on the beach at Manzanita. The massive ship listed to one side in the sand, exposing the gaping hole where it had been struck by cannon fire, while part of the deck had burned, and the torn sails suggested it had been through the mother of all storms. But the Jolly Roger, the skull and crossbones flag used by all pirates good and evil, still hung in tatters from the mast.

There would be treasure in the ship! Linden took off running across the sand, followed close behind by Bobby. They drew their swords in case pirates were still aboard. They crossed through the hole in the hull and it grew dark inside, but even so, they could see the glint of gold in the gloom. The rattle of chains or maybe skeletons came from farther up in the ship and—

"Wake up! For the love of all that is good in the world, WAKE UP!"

Linden lashed out with arms and legs to fight the evil green octopus stalking him through the woods. He leaped over a downed tree with Bobby close behind. They had their knives out, but the small blades were little protection against the poisonous fangs of the—

"WAKE UP! WAKE UP! WAKE UP!"

What the—where was he? He opened his eyes to stare into Willow's face.

"Oh, thank goodness," Willow said. "Why do you have to be so hard to wake up?"

"I was having this amazing dream," Linden said.

"There's no time for that. It's time to go back to Bannon Foods. Elon's already awake and dressed. Get ready and come downstairs."

Willow had gotten permission from their parents ahead of time. So this morning Linden found himself on the bus at five, a full three hours before he normally needed to be at school. He leaned against Willow, just for a moment, and the next thing he knew, Willow was shaking him awake again.

Still pitch-black out, they debarked a few blocks from Bannon Foods. The city was scary this early. They'd been here once before in daylight, but it was still mostly un-known, an industrial area of tall buildings, empty lots, and big trucks being loaded by people with harsh voices. He reached for Willow's hand, found her grasping for his. He looked across, saw that Elon was holding her other hand.

"Was this a good idea?" he said in a whisper.

"We told mom and dad we were visiting Bannon Foods to watch the truck loading. They were okay with it, so they must trust us to be able to handle the situation."

Linden nodded in the darkness full of strange sounds, but his heart thudded in his chest.

They passed the next-door property with the empty parking lot and warehouse set way back that Linden had mistaken for Bannon Foods on their first visit. Then they saw the Bannon Foods sign, lit by floodlights underneath.

They drew closer. The street was slightly elevated compared to the Bannon Foods parking lot, so they had a bird's-eye view of the warehouse. Every loading bay had a truck in it, and inside they could hear the roar of engines and backup alarms of many forklifts beeping. The warehouse had no windows, though, and they couldn't see a thing inside.

"We're going to have to wait for a truck to pull away, and then get into a position where we can see what's going on inside through the doorway."

"I have the license plate of Monday's delivery truck," Elon said, camera in one hand. "I got it while I was by the bike rack. Do you think they'll use the same truck?"

"The driver knew Miss Berry by her first name, and they were friendly," Willow said. "It must be the same driver every time."

"Then it's probably the same truck," Linden said.

Finally a truck pulled away, and they could see inside, but it was just a tiny sliver of the warehouse.

"Let's get closer," Elon said.

They left the chain-link fence by the street, and ran down the driveway into the lot, then snuck the last fifty feet.

"Wait," Elon said, taking a photo of the truck next to them. "This is it."

They stopped and stared. The truck's yellow paint was muted in the darkness.

"You sure?" Willow asked.

"Yes."

"Look!" Linden pointed up at the empty driver's cab, where they could see the silhouette of a doorway from the driver's cab into the cargo area. "If we get into the cab, we could see exactly what's being loaded, without going into the warehouse."

"Brilliant!" Willow gave him a quick hug. "Elon and I will go in, since he's got the camera. Can you keep lookout, Linden?"

Lookout? "What am I supposed to do?"

"Can you make a sound like a bird if you see someone coming?"

"Uh, no."

"Can you caw like a crow?"

"I don't think so."

"Can you bark like a dog?"

Linden thought for a moment and smiled. "Sure, I can do that."

Willow reached up for the handle on the truck, and gently pulled open the door. Elon climbed in and Willow followed, then they pulled the door mostly closed behind them, leaving it slightly ajar for a speedy escape.

Linden looked all around for a place to hide. He didn't want to be too close to a truck and accidentally get run over. But he had to see if someone was coming toward the cab where Willow and Elon were hiding. The edge of the building was one long loading dock, a ledge ten feet deep, with a door for each of the dozen trucks. He realized the ledge had an overhang of a few feet.

From under the overhang, he wouldn't be able to see anyone loading the truck, but he could see someone approaching the cab. And he'd be hidden from the workers above. He waited until the loading dock was clear, then scurried under the cover of darkness to the overhang. Squatting on his feet, he had a perfect view of the truck cab.

Overhead he heard the nonstop noise of loaders yelling to each other, radios squawking with instructions he didn't understand, and the ever-present movement of forklifts, their engines roaring and backup alarms beeping.

For all that, it was boring being the lookout. He'd gotten up too early, and he could feel himself growing sleepy again, even amid the background noise. His eyes drooped and closed once. He pinched himself awake. He had to keep the lookout.

There was a even louder grinding noise from above the platform, a continuous thunder that rattled the platform itself. He couldn't imagine what the noise was, so he risked a quick peek, and he realized it was one of the big metal doors coming down. He ducked back down into his hiding spot as a pair of boots approached.

Suddenly there was a thud right next to him as a driver jumped off the loading dock and strode toward the cab.

He had to give the signal. Oh, snap. The driver was right there, between Linden and the cab, and would hear the bark. But Linden didn't have a choice, he had to warn Elon and Willow for them to have a chance to get out. He took a deep breath, and then barked as loud as he could: RUFF! RUFF! RUFF!

The driver turned and stared at him.

Linden froze.

"What are you—"

Linden didn't wait to hear what he was going to say. He scrabbled under the ledge until he got to the opening between the next two trucks over, and then ran away.

He cleared the front of the trucks, and then veered to the right, toward the entrance.

Elon and Willow were right in front of them! They all ran as fast as they could, their sneakers slapping the ground, the wind blowing in their hair.

Distantly they heard a few shouts behind them, but they kept running as fast as they could, up the driveway, then down the street. They didn't want to stop in the neighborhood to catch a bus where the truck drivers might seem them when they left Bannon. They kept running, ten, fifteen, twenty blocks, until they finally pulled up gasping and sweating near a bus stop. They hid between a clump of trees, their hands on their knees as they tried to regain their breath.

"Well?" Linden finally asked between gasps.

"It's not the driver," Willow answered, straightening up and putting one hand on her ribs. "The food came on rotten."

Elon nodded. "We could see the driver talking to another driver. He didn't even do the loading. A bunch of other guys came and went. And they brought some nasty stuff on."

Linden felt himself flush and grow angry. "So what was the point of getting up so early? Nothing. We learned nothing about who's doing it."

"We learned the driver didn't," Willow said. "That's part of the process of elimination. We have to keep tracking it back further. We need to see where the guys loading it are getting it from."

"How are we going to do that?" Linden said. "We almost got caught as it was. We can't go inside the warehouse."

"Yeah, well, I have an idea about that," Elon said. "A way to watch them so that we can't get caught, and we can see everything they do."

CHAPTER SEVENTEEN

On Saturday morning their dad made chocolate chip pancakes, and when the kids finished breakfast, they holed up in the garage with the door closed for privacy.

"Tell us the plan again," Willow said.

"We use the drone," Elon explained. "We need to finish it up this weekend, get it all working perfectly by Sunday night, including the live camera feed. Then on Monday morning, we go back to Bannon Foods. Instead of going into their parking lot, we'll go to the place next door that's always been closed and set up there. Then we fly the drone over to Bannon Foods and into the warehouse.

We'll land it on the top of one of those big stacks of dry goods, with the camera pointing into the middle of the warehouse. Then we can watch everything they do from the inside, without being there ourselves."

Linden and Willow looked from Elon to the drone and back again.

"The Silver Dragon is pretty noisy," Linden said. "I think they'll hear it coming into the building."

"Did you hear how loud it was when they open and closed the metal doors at the loading dock?"

Linden nodded.

"We just have to fly it in under the cover of a door opening. Once we've landed inside, it'll be silent until we leave."

"I don't know," Willow said, shaking her head. "It sounds crazy. How quickly can we get it in a doorway and land it?"

"We'll have to practice," Elon said.

"What about the autopilot?" Linden asked "This is supposed to be an *autonomous* drone."

"The GPS won't work inside," Elon said.

"Dead reckoning?" Willow said. "Can't the motion sensors detect how far it's flown?"

Elon shook his head. "It's not exact. And besides, we don't have a perfect map of the inside of the building."

"What are you saying?" Willow said. "That'll you'll fly it by hand without even being able to see it?"

"We'll have the camera and your laptop," Elon said. "We can fly by watching the video feed."

"The camera's not working yet," Linden said.

"Then we get it to work," Elon said. "You do want to solve this mystery, right? And we built the quadcopter so we could do stuff with it. Imagine how good it'll look at the science fair if we catch a criminal!"

Willow and Linden slowly nodded.

"We're going to need supplies," Linden said. "Chocolate chip cookies. Potato chips."

"Root beer," Willow said. "And seaweed."

After they'd stockpiled the necessary nourishments, they all got to work.

Elon worked on mounting the camera, while Linden and Willow worked together on the camera telemetry module, the transmitter that would broadcast live video to Willow's laptop.

Willow and Linden argued over wireless protocols, while Elon placed the camera in a weatherproof housing, then attached it to the frame, where it hung off the leading edge. Staring at the lens, he knew it would unbalance the quadcopter. The autonomous leveler would keep the drone flat, but it'd be less efficient than being balanced. So he hung the drone from a string in the center, and moved the battery pack toward the back until the weight was symmetrical again.

It was hanging nicely from the string, and he was staring straight into the camera, when he noticed himself in a window on Willow's laptop.

"It's working!" he cried.

"It's working!" he heard from Willow's laptop a fraction of a second later.

"There's audio, too!" he said in surprise.

"There's audio, too!" came from the laptop.

"One high-def video and audio stream," Linden called.

"Sweet." Elon put one hand on the drone, and turned it slightly so it was pointed out the window. The big Douglas fir in the yard appeared on Willow's laptop. "Are we done?"

"We still need to wire up the avoidance detectors."

The drone had five ultrasonic range finders. Each was accurate to within inches. One faced down, and the others were pointed in each of the four directions. They'd connected the downward-facing range finder so they could maintain a constant altitude. The other four were to make sure the drone didn't crash into anything.

"Do we need them for Monday?" Elon asked.

"Depends," Linden answered, "on whether you want to crash into any forklifts, support poles, or boxes inside the warehouse."

"Good point."

By the afternoon they'd finished wiring it all together.

Then they took it for a test flight in the yard with the last light of day. With avoidance detection and stabilization, it was tame enough to control even in their small yard.

"Tomorrow we practice flying around obstacles," Elon said.

"More important than that," Willow said, "is that we have to fly using only the video on my camera. You can't be out here where you can see the yard. You've got to do it all using only my laptop."

Elon stared at the screen and thought about the difficulty of controlling the quadcopter when he could see in just one direction at a time. "Oh, snap."

Sunday came in a blink, and they spent the day in a haze of debugging, tuning, and test flights.

They set up an obstacle course to mimic what they thought it would be like to fly inside the warehouse. Linden was stationed outside so he could let Elon know if he was about to crash. Willow and Elon set up inside the garage, with the laptop and controller. It turned out they couldn't hear a thing over the drone's audio while it was in flight due to the noise of the rotors, so they used walkie-talkies to communicate.

By the end of the day, Elon could fly the copter through the swing set, around the Douglas fir, between the cherry trees, and then land it on top of the minivan in the driveway.

"Ninety seconds," Willow said, shaking her head.

"That's good." Elon shook out his hands, which were shaky and sweating after hours of flights. But he felt confident that he could do it tomorrow.

"Except the loading-bay doors only took like a minute to go up and down, so people are going to hear the buzz. And you've never flown inside the actual warehouse. You knew which way to bank and turn here."

Elon shook his head, afraid he might cry. "I'm doing the best I can!"

"I know, I know," she said, putting her arm around him. "We'll just have to do what we can."

Linden stood in the doorway carrying the quadcopter. "I have an idea. Doesn't Atlanta's dad have an air horn from those races he judged? That could cover up the sound of the Silver Dragon, and maybe distract anyone from looking where it's going."

They all nodded slowly.

"That could work," Willow said. She looked outside. "It's getting late. I'd better ride over there right away."

"Wait!" Elon rushed for his camera. "Let's all get a picture with it."

They gathered around the project table, with the Silver Dragon parked on the surface. Willow held her laptop, and Linden the remote control. Elon set the camera for an auto-picture, then ran around and got in the middle, his arms around his siblings. The flash went off with blaze of light, then Elon checked the photo. Perfect!

Willow left in a rush, and Linden and Elon set all the batteries to charge. They packed the Silver Dragon inside a cardboard box, because they'd have to take it on the bus first thing in the morning.

When Willow got back with the air horn, she packed her laptop and the remote control.

"Basil and Atlanta are almost done with their science-fair project," Willow said. "They've got twenty feet of hair-rope, and they built a wood swing set, so people will be able to sit on it and swing. Even Atlanta's dad sat on it and swung."

"Whoa," Linden said.

"It's gonna be cool," Willow said. "But I'm still glad we worked on the drone. We couldn't be doing what we're going to do tomorrow morning without it. Good idea, Elon."

"Yeah, great idea!" Linden said.

Elon smiled, tired but happy that the autonomous drone worked and their plan to spy on Bannon Foods had come together.

CHAPTER EIGHTEEN

They arrived once more at the stop near Bannon Foods. Willow's backpack was heavy with her laptop inside its protective sleeve. Linden's bag also sagged under the weight of batteries and controller, while Elon struggled to fit the light but large cardboard box with the drone through the bus's door.

They kept to the shadows as they approached Bannon even earlier than they'd ever gotten there before. A long row of trucks were parked in front of the loading bays. But unlike their prior visits, when the parking lot was nearly full, this time there was only one car parked in the lot and the warehouse doors were shut.

"Thank goodness," Linden said. "They do sleep like normal people."

"I'm glad they're not undead," Elon said, "because then they'd never sleep."

Willow shushed them. "We don't want anyone to look up here."

They turned into the property next to Bannon Foods, a small brown industrial building with its own parking lot, where they'd never seen more than a few cars. They found an area on the side nearest Bannon. They set up between two garbage dumpsters, carefully unpacking the Silver Dragon, plugging in batteries, and getting the accessories ready. The backlight off Willow's laptop hurt their eyes in the darkness of the night, so Willow turned the brightness way down.

"It's good for battery life, too."

Linden got out the binoculars, laid on his stomach at the edge of the parking lot, and tried to read license plate numbers on the trucks. He couldn't see anything, so he got out his dad's Tiablo flashlight, and focused the narrow beam at the bumper of the first truck. The fancy LED light had a brightness control, so he dialed it down to a mere one percent to start. He had to increase to three percent power before he could see anything, but then the light bounced off the reflective license plate, and he could read it. He went down the line of trucks as fast as he could, knowing that even the tight beam, low-light flashlight would give away his position if anyone looked up. When he got to the fifth truck, the plate matched.

"It's fifth from the left," he explained.

"Got it," Willow said.

Everything was ready, so they turned the drone on, connected the wireless, and checked the video feed on Willow's laptop. Elon overlaid the flight-planning software with a satellite map of the area. He marked their current location. He looked across the lot with binoculars, picked out a flat spot on the roof of Bannon's warehouse, then programmed that location into Willow's computer. He glanced at Willow, who nodded, so he clicked start on the flight plan.

The copter's rotors spun, blades slicing the air with a startling loud whine in the night. Resisting the urge to watch the drone itself, he kept his eyes focused on the screen to watch the video feed from the camera. The drone flew itself toward the warehouse, but Elon kept his hands on the controls, ready to override the autopilot if necessary.

The lights off the Bannon warehouse silhouetted the dark trucks parked in front. The copter flew past a truck, then rose up over the lip of the building roof, and settled down. As soon as the drone landed, Elon cut the throttle to save batteries and avoid noise. From the rooftop, it would be a short, quick flight into the building.

Elon programmed the next set of waypoints, his fingers flying over the keyboard in the darkness. He knew roughly where the pallet racks were inside the warehouse, and he'd only need to take control at the last moment to land.

They didn't have long to wait. Suddenly the far left loading-dock door began to open, a dull roar even at this distance.

"Wait," Willow said. "They'll be looking at that door. Go when the next door starts to open."

Elon nodded.

When the door was halfway up, the next one started to open, and when that was halfway up, the third one opened.

"Perfect," Linden said. "They've got twelve doors to open, so you'll have at least five minutes of noise cover to get into position."

Elon engaged the autopilot, and it followed the waypoints he set. The drone rose up off the roof, dipped down as soon as it passed the ledge, and flew through the doorway. With no GPS inside the building, the drone would have to fly the last little bit using motion sensors.

They followed its progress on the laptop screen, watching from its point of view, as it swooped through the top of the doorway, then turned abruptly left, and rose up to within a few feet of the ceiling and flew forward thirty feet. Then it stopped, hovering in midair.

"This is where I have to fly it," Elon said. He spotted a tall pallet rack a few feet away, flew up and over. He checked the telemetry window to make sure he was centered over a pallet, and set the throttle to zero. The copter settled down with a thump.

The big garage doors continued their rolling thunder as the video screen showed nothing but a blank wall.

"It's facing the wrong way!" Willow practically jumped up.

"Relax," Elon said. He set the altitude for three inches, then gave the rudder control short taps until the drone turned and faced toward the doors.

Now they saw the long line of open doorways on the right side of the screen. In the middle of the dozen doors stood a man flipping switches one by one and watching the doors open. He gave no sign of having seen the Silver Dragon enter. In the middle of the screen, a long row of forklifts sat parked. Toward the left side of the screen they saw the massive refrigerator.

"Perfect," Willow said in a hushed whisper. She started recording the video and turned up the laptop sound, so they could hear what was happening in the warehouse. For a few minutes more, they heard only the rumbling of doors.

When the last door opened, the figure walked away from the switches.

"Is that Mr. Hutchins, the foreman?" Linden asked.

"I can't tell," Willow said. "He's just a little bit too far away to make out the details. Maybe he'll come closer."

But he didn't come closer. In fact, he went farther away, towards the far end of the long row of doors. He got really small on the screen.

"Maybe I should move the drone closer," Elon said.

"No, we don't want to risk the noise now."

The man - at least they thought he was from his short hair, clothes, and the way he walked - stopped at the last door. His arms waved back and forth, and he turned and pointed toward the refrigerator.

"That does look like Mr. Hutchins," Linden said. "Look at the way his arms are waving around."

"He talks with his hands, Mom would say," Willow remembered, from the last time they met him.

Mr. Hutchins then walked toward the left side of the screen where the offices were and disappeared off-camera. Soon after, two figures with handtrucks unloaded boxes from the far truck and brought them closer to the camera, toward the middle of the screen.

Suddenly the first man reappeared and opened the big refrigerator door. The two workers brought the boxes into the refrigerator, stacking them in a pile right next to the door, and then went back toward their truck.

"OMG," Elon said. "This is boring. Are we really going to watch people move stuff all morning?"

"We have no choice," Willow said.

For fifteen more minutes, they watched workers move food. Some boxes went into the refrigerator, adding to the pile next to the door. Others got stacked in various places around the warehouse. Mr. Hutchins came out a last time to talk to the workers, handing them something, and they gave him a tan folder and went back to their truck.

Willow heard the engine start. "See if you can get their license plate, and if it says anything on their door, like the name of the company."

Linden nodded, then ran towards the driveway, keeping low. He noticed a few cars pulling into the Bannon Foods lot, then he heard the rumble of the truck leaving. The old blue truck came slowly up the driveway, its engine laboring as it climbed the incline to street level. It was impossible to read the faded letters on the side of the truck in the light coming off the street lamp. But he risked using the flashlight again for a brief moment to get the license plate, then scurried back to the others.

"Got the license plate, but I couldn't make out the company name. It was from California. The truck was blue. And now some other employees are showing up to work. What's happening inside?"

"Nothing," Willow said. "Mr. Hutchins went into the back."

A few minutes later, the new employees entered the picture. They spoke with Mr. Hutchins, closer to the camera on the drone, and this time they could make out for sure that it was him.

"Does this mean Mr. Hutchins is the one who is responsible?" Elon asked.

"We didn't see him do anything wrong," Linden said. "He was just here at work, early, receiving a delivery."

"Yes, but look at that!" Willow said. She pointed to a pile of black plastic crates on-screen. "I've been watching, and that's one of the things unloaded from the blue truck. If it gets loaded onto the truck for our school, we'll know exactly where it came from."

Another fifteen minutes passed, and finally they saw a worker load the boxes into the Mt. Hood Elementary truck. By this time, some of the other yellow Bannon Foods trucks had already departed. From where they sat, they could see new trucks in a variety of colors arriving and then idling in the long driveway, waiting to unload new deliveries, the big refrigeration units above their cabs rumbling to keep the contents cold.

"The blue truck wasn't a Bannon Foods truck," Linden mused.

"Right. We know that. It was delivering food," Willow said.

"It also didn't have one of those things above the cab."

"They call it a reefer, short for refrigerator," Willow said. "Mrs. Dozen talked about them in class."

"But we saw them put the food from the blue truck into the refrigerator in the warehouse. So it was food that was supposed to be refrigerated!" Linden said.

"Oh!" Willow rubbed her eyes. "That is suspicious."

"So we have an early-morning delivery before any of the regular workers arrived," Elon said, taking his eyes off the screen. "That Mr. Hutchins personally supervised. It came on an unrefrigerated truck, when we know it should be refrigerated. We know that food went to Mt. Hood Elementary."

"I wish we could see what was in the crate," Willow said. "We don't have a zoom on this camera?"

Elon and Linden shook their heads.

"I have to fly it out at some point," Elon said. "So I could do it now and fly past the back of the truck to get a close up view."

"Okay, program the waypoints."

"I can't," Elon said. "No GPS in there and the motion sensors aren't accurate enough to find the doorway. I'll have to fly it by hand. Here goes." Elon started the rotors, and slid the drone forward, then down. He flew toward the truck, then stopped and hovered for just a moment in front of it. They got a clear view of the black plastic crates.

"Wilted broccoli!" Willow cried, pointing at the screen. "I knew it. That's it!"

Elon pressed forward to fly the copter out into the parking lot.

"Wait!" Willow put one hand on his arm. "I want to know what those workers put into the refrigerator. Fly toward the refrigerator."

"There's workers all over. They'll see us, if they haven't already."

"We need to know."

"*Fine!*" Elon yelled, though his tone made it clear that it wasn't fine with him at all. "We're risking the Silver Dragon by doing this."

He did a quick one-eighty, then flew at top speed toward the refrigerator door, which was open. Workers everywhere stopped what they were doing and looked up toward the silver and black copter now roaring through the warehouse. As it got to the doorway, Elon centered the control stick, and the Silver Dragon stopped dead in its tracks, hovering. The camera centered on the pile of boxes next to the door, the boxes they'd seen unloaded from the unrefrigerated truck that morning.

"Sliced beef!?" Willow screamed. "You have to refrigerate meat!"

"Get out," Linden said. "Get out!" He pointed at the screen, where someone was rushing toward the copter waving a broomstick in the air.

Elon reversed the copter, flying backwards, away from the approaching figure. He did another one-eighty turn to fly toward the doors, but as the camera panned around, they saw another figure approaching with a fire extinguisher.

He banked left and almost ran into a pole, then veered around it. A man threw handfuls of carrots at the drone. The drone dove forward at maximum speed, its rotors sending up a cloud of white dust as it passed over the flour repacking station.

Mr. Hutchins was visibly waving his arms and yelling, even though he was inaudible under the scream of the four rotors at top power. He picked up a plastic crate and threw it toward the drone.

"The folder!" Willow yelled. "Next to Mr. Hutchins is the tan folder he got from the people on the blue truck. It's open. We need to see what it says."

Elon continued to fly maneuvers, dodging obstacles, thrown objects, and people.

"Uh," Linden said. "Too much. Just get out."

"It's evidence," Willow said.

"Fine," Elon grunted. He did another about-face, and flew straight at Mr. Hutchins.

Mr. Hutchkin's eyes went big and he dove for the floor.

Elon flipped a switch, tilting the drone forward and hitting negative throttle, spinning the rotors backwards. For a brief second, the Silver Dragon hung motionless in the air, sideways to the ground, so that the forward-facing camera faced straight down to the sheets of paper below. In a fraction of a second, the drone fell toward the ground, then Elon hit regular throttle again and took off toward the flour station.

Workers from everywhere ran toward the drone, carrying brooms, boxes, potatoes, and fire extinguishers. The drone hovered above a giant open bag of flour, its powerful fan blades sending up billowing clouds of white dust so thick no one could see in. Elon waited for several seconds, then dove forward again, flying out of the cloud.

None of the workers were ready, and he flew right past them, before they could react. None except for Mr. Hutchins, who suddenly rose up from the ground and threw a broom like a spear toward the copter.

The boom handle passed right into the blade guard for the right front rotor. The rotor, spinning hundreds of times per second, hit the broomstick and snapped clean off as the weight of the heavy boom brought the Silver Dragon crashing to the ground.

"NOOO!" Elon yelled as Linden and Willow stared in shock.

CHAPTER NINETEEN

Elon stood up, like he was going to run into Bannon Foods but Willow and Linden grabbed him at the same time to hold him back.

"We can't go in there," Linden yelled.

"But the drone!" Elon's eyes turned red.

"I know," Willow said. "We just have to —"

Whatever she was going to say never got said because Mr. Hutchins came to the loading bay and looked out. The day had brightened after sunrise, and though they were several hundred feet away, Mr. Hutchins saw them clearly.

"Hey, kids—what the heck are you doing?" he bellowed. He turned and yelled something into the warehouse, and suddenly he and several workers starting running toward them, yelling for the kids to stay where they were.

Mr. Hutchins' group would have to run up the long Bannon driveway filled with delivery trucks and then around the chain-link fence. But there was no doubt they were coming for them.

"We have to get out of here," Willow said, slamming shut her laptop. "We recorded the video. It's evidence. We can't let them get a hold of it."

She slid the computer inside her backpack as Elon and Linden roughly shoved all the other gear into their backpacks. They took off at a run, out of the adjoining property, and onto the street.

They beat Mr. Hutchins and the other workers to the street, and pealed out down the sidewalk.

Their backpacks slammed up and down on their shoulders as they ran. The heavy bags loaded with gear slowed them down. When Linden glanced back, he saw Mr. Hutchins and two other workers half a block behind them.

"Run faster," Linden gasped. "They're gaining."

They put on another small burst of energy, even as Linden saw the tears still coming down Elon's face.

"I want the Silver Dragon back!" Elon yelled as tears streamed down his face.

"We'll get it," Willow promised. "Somehow. But we have to get away, or they'll take my laptop and then we'll have no proof and it will all be for nothing."

Their energy started to flag several blocks on, and Mr. Hutchins's group grew closer, less than a hundred feet away.

"What do we do?" Willow cried.

"Bobby, trip them!" Linden yelled.

Willow yelled back, "BOBBY IS NOT—"

A thud behind them caused them to all look back. Mr. Hutchins had tripped, and his coworkers were helping him up.

"Huh," Willow said.

"The streetcar!" Linden gasping for breath and pointing to the end of the block. "It's pulling in."

Indeed, the Portland streetcar was slowing at a stop less than a block away.

"Time for warp nine, guys," Willow said, sweat streaking down her face.

The streetcar stopped, people got off and on. Linden, Willow, and Elon raced up as the doors started to close. They dashed inside, their backpacks nearly caught in the doorway.

Linden's vision was starting to go dark, and he couldn't hear a thing over the blood pounding in his ears. But he looked up with alarm when something slammed against the door just inches away. His heart beat even harder as he realized that Mr. Hutchins stood outside banging on the glass door!

The streetcar slowly pulled away, Mr. Hutchins running alongside and banging on the door, until it outpaced him and left him behind.

Linden dropped onto a seat in exhaustion and shock. "Holy cow."

Willow and Elon plopped down next to him.

Willow's face had gone white. "I think I almost got us all killed."

Elon wiped tears away with one sleeve. "How are we going to get the drone back?"

Willow turned and hugged him. "We'll do everything we can. If we have to, we'll build it from scratch."

"But the science fair is this Friday!"

Willow shook her head. "I know you're just thinking about the drone, but look at the evidence we gathered. We have to go right to the principal's office. Once we get that taken of, we'll figure out what to do."

Elon hugged his legs and didn't speak for the rest of the way to school.

CHAPTER TWENTY

Willow arrived at school with her brothers in tow. She had tried to comfort Elon, who was still despondent over the loss of the drone, and Linden, who was generally terrified, but she was so in shock herself, she felt drained.

As they walked up the stairs at the main entrance of Mt. Hood Elementary, parents and other kids stopped and stared at them.

Willow glanced down at herself and her brothers. They were sweaty, covered in grease and dirt from the parking lot, and completely disheveled from their long run from Mr. Hutchins. She'd somehow ripped her second-favorite pair of leggings.

She held her head up high, grabbed her brothers' hands, and stalked up the stairs to the main office.

She stood in the front of the long counter until the office manager noticed her and came over.

"We need to see Principal Winterson immediately," Willow said. "It's...a matter of life and death."

The manager looked the three of them up and down. "Come with me."

She led them through the room to the side door of the principal's office. She knocked twice, then opened the door. "Mrs. Winterson, these students need to see you right away."

"Send them in," Mrs. Winterson said.

They entered together and the door closed behind then. They stood standing in front of the principal's desk. She sat, fingers interlaced, and waited for them to talk.

The silence lingered on, but suddenly Willow was afraid to speak. What if the principal didn't believe her? What if Mr. Hutchins was waiting outside to kill them? What if they'd broken some law when they spied on the warehouse, and had to go to jail? What if they were wrong about everything? What were her parents going to say?

She opened her mouth, but no words would come to her.

Linden looked at her, then cleared his throat. "Mrs. Winterson, you may be aware that some students have been getting sick. Willow noticed that it was only certain kids and only on certain days."

"Is that so?" Mrs. Winterson looked directly at Willow.

"That's true," she said, in a whisper. She took a breath and forced herself to speak in a bigger voice. "Only those kids who ate hot lunch on Mondays and Thursdays."

"I know that we've had a stomach flu going around, but I'm sure that affects all children equally." Mrs. Winterson looked off in the distance for a second. "You're friends with Atlanta, aren't you? Are you concerned about her going to the hospital?"

"It's not that, Mrs. Winterson." Willow had to convince her. "I mean, I am worried about Atlanta. But we have evidence. Video evidence. It's here on my laptop."

She slid the computer out of her backpack and put it on the principal's desk without waiting for permission. She started the video they'd recorded that morning. "It shows that Bannon Foods, the food distributor who supplies our cafeteria food, received unrefrigerated food via a truck from California, then placed it in their refrigerator, and they'll be delivering it here this morning and claiming it's local food. It's not, Mrs. Winterson. I don't know exactly what's going on, but it's something weird."

The principal watched a few minutes of the video, then paused it, and hit a button on her desk phone. "Get me Miss Berry from the cafeteria and the assistant principal. Have them report to my office."

Soon the other adults arrived. "Start that from the beginning, Willow," the principal said.

At the end of the video, Willow was asked to explain everything. "It started with Mrs. Dozen's class on how food gets to us. We talked about local foods, and then I went to dinner one night at a restaurant and saw local food, real local food, and I knew what we were getting in the cafeteria wasn't it." She went on to explain all the steps of their investigation: visiting Bannon Foods, watching the truck delivery, and spying on the warehouse.

Miss Berry nodded throughout Willow's explanation.

"I told you, Miriam," she said to the principal. "I said something was wrong with our food delivery."

"I'm sorry, Ada," Mrs. Winterson said. "I just figured the food wasn't quite up to snuff. I didn't realize the situation was so bad." She turned to face the kids. "I'm going to call the police, and then we're going to visit Bannon Foods."

Soon they were driving to Bannon Foods in the back of Mrs. Winterson's car, with Miss Berry in the passenger seat. The principal had a grim look on her face the whole drive over.

A police car was parked in the lot at Bannon Foods, a uniformed officer waiting next to the door.

"I'm Officer Whitmarsh," she said, one hand held out.

"You'll accompany me inside," Mrs. Winterson said, without breaking stride.

They entered the building, trailing Mrs. Winterson.

"Do you know what's going on?" Officer Whitmarsh asked Willow, turning in beside her.

"They're giving our school cafeteria bad food," she said. "The evidence is here on my laptop."

Linden and Elon followed so close behind they kept giving her flat tires.

"Sorry," Linden said to Willow. Then he turned to the police officer and held out a scrap of paper. "We've got the license plate for the truck that delivered the spoiled food."

Officer Whitmarsh took the paper, scooped up her radio from her belt, and asked for a license-plate check.

Mrs. Winterson stormed passed Brett's desk and went right into Tom Bannon's office. Miss Berry, Officer Whitmarsh, Elon, Linden, and Willow all followed.

CHAPTER TWENTY-ONE

Tom Bannon sat at his desk, his phone held to one ear. The door to his office blew open and the crowd entered.

"Bob, I'm going to have to get back to you. I think I have an emergency." Mr. Bannon hung up, and stood. "Hello? How can I help you?"

Elon realized that if Mr. Hutchins saw them all here, he might try to make a getaway. He reached out for Officer Whitmarsh, and pulled her down close, even as he heard Mrs. Winterson explaining what happened.

"We think Mr. Hutchins, the warehouse foreman, is

in on it. He's in the back," Elon said, and went on to explain what he looked like.

Officer Whitmarsh listened for a moment more, then rushed out through the office door.

Mr. Bannon was pale and his hands shook. As Miss Berry and Mrs. Winterson continued their accusations, Mr. Bannon sank into his seat.

"We've never done anything wrong," Mr. Bannon said. "I inherited this company from my father and grandfather. We've been in business for over fifty years. There just has to be a mistake."

Willow cleared her throat and everyone looked at her. "The Monday delivery to the school is supposed to include our local food, right?"

Mr. Bannon nodded. "Yes, we discussed this when you visited."

"Then what do you make of this?" Willow turned her laptop around so that it faced Mr. Bannon. It was that morning's video feed, paused on an image of a sheet of paper. "The photo is blurry, but you can see white paper on a tan folder—the same folder we saw Mr. Hutchins receive this morning from the workers unloading the blue truck. The food from that truck then got loaded onto the truck for Mt. Hood Elementary."

"I can't read the text," Mr. Bannon said. "It's too blurry."

"But can you read the company letterhead at the top?" Willow asked.

"Los Angeles Distribution Services." Mr. Bannon's voice was weak.

"Los Angeles, California is not within four hundred miles of Portland," Willow said. "So that food is not local. It also wasn't refrigerated, even though it's a fourteen-hour drive from LA."

Mr. Bannon shook his head. "It doesn't make sense. I've never even heard of them, let alone done business with them."

"Maybe he has," Officer Whitmarsh said, accompanied by Mr. Hutchins.

"What's going on here, Tom?" Mr. Hutchins said, nodding politely to each of the adults in the room. When he laid eyes on the kids, he stopped smiling and clenched his jaw.

Elon was ready for Mr. Hutchins to mention the spying that morning. But when seconds passed and Mr. Hutchins said nothing, he realized it was further evidence that Mr. Hutchins was guilty. He didn't want to say anything.

"Jack, has there been any problems with the Mt. Hood Elementary orders?" Mr. Bannon asked. "They're here because the food they've been receiving hasn't been fresh."

Miss Berry snorted at this understatement.

"No, it's been fine, Tom. We sent out the order this morning."

"You sure?" Mr. Bannon said. "Then what's this about an early-morning delivery from Los Angeles Distribution Services? A delivery that got loaded onto the school's truck."

Mr. Hutchins's eyes opened wide and his nose flared. "I don't know what that is. We delivered the same thing we always do to the school. Produce from two farms on Sauvie Island and meat from the Oregon Co-Op.

"No way," Willow said. "I went out for dinner with my parents, and we ate real local food and it is NOTHING like what's being served at school."

"Yeah," Elon said. "You're probably taking the food for the school and selling it to fancy restaurants!"

"Then you got some really cheap food," Linden said, "and delivered the cheap stuff to school, figuring that nobody would know the difference."

"What the—" Mr. Hutchins cut himself off, looking nervous. "Look, I have to get back to work in the back. I've got trucks to unload." He turned toward the door.

Officer Whitmarsh stepped in front, blocking his way. "I think you should wait right here until we're done."

Mr. Hutchins turned to face Elon, Willow, and Linden, nervousness turning to anger. "You nosy kids are making a big deal out of nothing."

Mrs. Winterson spoke up. "My students have laboriously gathered evidence to the contrary. They show the delivery this morning, the packing of the foods onto the truck, the paperwork. What are you trying to hide, Mr. Hutchins?"

Tom Bannon reached up and smacked his forehead with one hand. "Hutchins, does this have anything to do with Better Business Bureau complaints filed against us since my father died? We had other customers complain. How could I be so foolish? You took advantage of me, because I didn't know as much about the business as my father."

Mr. Hutchins nearly shook with anger and his face grew a dark red. He looked like he was going to say something, then shook his head slightly, and changed his mind. His shoulders slumped. "I want to speak to my lawyer," he said.

Officer Whitmarsh smiled at that. "Fine. You can call your lawyer down at the police station. I'll need you to come with me." She turned to Mr. Bannon. "I'll call for a couple of detectives to come down and look at the warehouse, so touch as little as possible."

Mr. Bannon nodded, then turned to the rest of the group. He rubbed one hand through his hair.

"I am real sorry for whatever has happened. You've been our customer for years, and I will do whatever it takes to make it up to you. I'll get a truck loaded right now with our best stuff."

"Thank you, Mr. Bannon," Miss Berry said. "That would be very nice."

"Mr. Bannon?" Elon asked.

"Yes?"

"Our drone, which we used to take the video, is here in your warehouse. Mr. Hutchins attacked it with a broom. Can we look for it? It's our science-fair project."

"Of course," Mr. Bannon said, and led them into the warehouse.

They found the Silver Dragon in Mr. Hutchins's office in the back. They could see it laying there on his desk, the rotor broken and the case cracked.

Elon wanted to run to it, but Mr. Bannon blocked his way with one arm, gentle but firm.

"The police are probably going to want to go in there, so we shouldn't touch a thing."

Elon's heart sank. Willow put one arm around him and Linden took his hand.

"We'll figure something out," Linden said.

CHAPTER TWENTY-TWO

The week until the science fair passed quickly.

On Monday, they got back to school with Mrs. Winterson by the middle of the morning. Before lunch, a new Bannon Foods truck showed up along with two chefs that Mr. Bannon had hired himself to help Miss Berry. Lunch was an enormous Italian meal, with fresh-made local pasta, meatballs, and right-out-of-the-oven Italian bread and garlic bread. The pasta was so good that even Linden abandoned the lunch he'd brought to get the hot lunch. And there was cake for dessert, even though the school wasn't really supposed to provide dessert.

Mrs. Winterson called Elon, Linden and Willow to her office right before the end of the day. She was sitting behind her desk, just as intimidating as usual. "Mr. Hutchins has been officially arrested by the police."

They nodded solemnly, not sure of what to say.

"You did a good job investigating the crime," the principal said.

"Thank you," they said in unison, then smiled at each other.

"More importantly," Mrs. Winterson went on, taking a deep breath, "you did the *right* thing. You investigated when no one else believed anything was wrong, and you kept investigating even when we didn't believe you, until you had the evidence. You may have saved people's lives and at least saved them from missing any more school."

Then the bell rang dismissing everyone. Mrs. Winterson looked like she wanted to say more, then changed her mind. "Go on, I know you want to go."

"Thank you, Mrs. Winterson," Willow said. "Thanks for believing us when we came in this morning."

Mrs. Winterson nodded, and they all filed out of her office in an orderly fashion, until they reached the hallway. Then they peeled out for the schoolyard.

The decadent meals continued. On Tuesday, the lunch was turkey pot pie, mac and cheese, stuffed artichokes, and brownies for dessert. On Wednesday, Linden decided he'd try hot lunch again. There was a cheese, sausage, and bread plate, olives, and bruschetta with fresh mozzarella, tomato, and basil. Dessert was gelato they made in class from fresh ingredients.

Late Wednesday night, as they sat around the dining room table doing homework, the phone rang. Mom answered it, and called Elon. Linden and Willow watched with surprise, as Elon didn't get many phone calls. He took it in the kitchen, and listened at first, then asked questions too quietly for Linden and Willow to overhear until he finally hung up a few minutes later.

He came into the dining room, and Linden and Willow pretended they hadn't been trying to listen in. Elon cleared his throat, and they both looked up.

"We won't be getting the Silver Dragon back. It's been confiscated as evidence by the police. They expect they'll need it until the trial is finished."

He sat down heavily in his chair, his chin resting on his hands.

"What are we going to do for the science fair?" Willow said.

They sat quietly for a moment.

"We'll just have to do a good poster," Linden said.

They started that evening, laying out the stand-up poster they'd use. They took turns drawing an intricate diagram of the quadcopter, starting with pencil, then overlaying with black marker, and coloring it in. Willow suggested they blow up the photo of the three of them with the drone they'd taken in the garage after they finished building it and before they'd taken it out to fly.

By Thursday, word had gotten back to Mr. Bannon that he'd forgotten it was a Japanese immersion school, and fresh sushi showed up. They had salmon *nigiri*, *onigiri*, *unagi*, and *udon* noodles. Dessert was *mochi* with red bean paste.

That night they put the finishing touches on their presentation and practiced what they'd say with their parents.

On Friday they had bento boxes of teriyaki chicken or salmon, pickled vegetables called *tsukimono*, rice, and dessert was fried ice cream.

And then before anyone realized it, it was Friday night, the science fair.

The cafeteria, which doubled as the auditorium, was hot and busy when they arrived back at school at six o'clock. Students and parents ran around, frantically setting up experiments. Electrolysis of water into hydrogen and oxygen was next to an experiment to measure the voltage from a potato battery.

Basil and Atlanta's project was so immense, they'd gotten placed by themselves on the stage. The large wooden structure was fifteen feet tall, their rope swing hanging from the crossbar. Atlanta stood on a tall ladder, attaching the human-hair braid to large eye-bolts. Atlanta's dad brought a wheelbarrow in, and together

Basil, Atlanta, and their parents carried sandbags onto the stage for the four corners of the structure.

The attention of the entire crowd was focused on the hive of activity around Basil and Atlanta's construction project.

"We're in the back," Willow said, holding the map of project locations in front of her. Linden and Elon followed her, Linden carrying the poster and Elon bringing a small crate of the spare parts they hadn't used in the drone. Linden stood up the poster board. Elon set out the parts with their accompanying labels, a half-dozen in all: two rotors, some wiring, an extra motor that didn't work, the transmitter.

They stepped back. The left-hand side of the poster was the line drawing they'd made together of the design of the Silver Dragon, showing each of the parts and its function. The right-hand side featured a printout of the photograph of them with the finished drone. The parts on the table didn't even fill the space.

They were sandwiched between kindergarteners with a baking-soda-and-vinegar volcano and second graders who'd put different foods in closed glass jars, and then left them for a month to see what would open. Every so often, they'd open a jar to give someone a sniff, and the whole area would be overcome with noxious odors.

Some kids ran by without a glance, talking about the liquid-nitrogen display down the aisle.

Willow sighed.

"I imagined we'd have the drone here, hovering above the crowd," Elon said, "picking things up, and carrying them around. It was going to be more impressive."

"If only we could have gotten it back," Linden said. "Even if we didn't fix it, at least there'd be something for people to see."

"It doesn't look like much," Willow agreed. "Let's go see Basil and Atlanta's project."

There was a thick cluster of kids surrounding the swing structure.

Basil stood on a chair to be seen over the crowd. He picked up an orange traffic cone and shouted into the thin end to amplify his voice. "Ride the world's first human hair swing. Feel the incredible strength. Braided from the hair of one thousand cheerleaders. Step right up. The line forms on the right. Come on now, don't be shy."

The crowd shuffled to the right, leaving a clear line of sight between Willow and Atlanta.

"Cool!" Willow said. "Can I have a turn?"

Atlanta beamed. "It's awesome isn't it? Basil—let Willow and her brothers go."

Basil nodded and bowed toward them with a gracious wave of his hand. "Ladies and germs first."

Willow sat down, grasping the rope on either side of her. It was coarse, with little strands poking out here and there. She could see brown hair, blonde hair, bits of black hair, even purple, blue, and pink streaks here and there. "Are you sure this can hold me?"

"We tested it with me, Atlanta, and my mom and dad at the same time, and my dad was even holding Bermuda." Bermuda was their great dane. "All together we weighed over six hundred pounds, and we jumped up and down."

Basil gave Willow a big push and she flew up into the air. With each additional push, she went higher and higher, until she was nearly horizontal to the ground. A big smile spread across her face as the wind blew through her hair. Then Basil slowed her down after just a couple of swings. "Sorry, but there's a lot of people waiting."

"No problem," she said. "That was awesome! *Arigatou gozaimasu*." Thank you.

"*Dou itashi mashite*," you're welcome, he replied, bowing his head. "Next!" he called, and Elon ran up.

Willow wandered back toward her exhibit. Still no one came to see what they'd done. Most of the kids were up at the hair-swing. Well, it was no wonder. Atlanta did have a great idea, and Basil had done an excellent job putting most of it together while Atlanta was sick, and they deserved all the attention. Still, Willow wished their drone would have at least gotten some notice.

Elon joined her, followed by Linden, once they'd gotten their turns on the swing. Soon after, there was a squealing from the PA system as the microphone was turned on. Mrs. Winterson took the stage, glancing behind her with some alarm at the towering swing structure. "Good evening students, parents, relatives and friends. Thank you for coming to our school science fair. As you know..."

Willow tuned out the speech, and looked around. Holy cow, there was a working laser beam on the next aisle over! She decided to leave her station to go see the laser when she felt a tug on her arm.

She looked next to her. Linden was pointing at the stage.

The big projector screen had come down, and the projector flashed white on the screen. Principal Winterson stood to one side of the screen. "One of the science-fair projects this term was of particular importance. Some of you may have heard that we had certain problems with the cafeteria food and students were taken ill. Thanks to the deductive skills of Willow, Elon, and Linden, the mystery of the school lunches was solved. Their science-fair project was an autonomous drone." Here even Mrs. Winterson stumbled slightly over the unusual words. "They used this drone to trace the food supply chain back towards its source. In doing so, they identified criminal activities. They used their drone to record an instrumental video that led to an arrest by the police. Without further ado, I'd like to show you this video, and afterwards you may ask them any questions you like about their project."

With that, the room lights dimmed, and the video started. The video began with a short test flight of the drone. The Silver Dragon flew in their yard. It turned toward their workshop window, and for a few moments, they could see the reflection of the drone in the dark window. Then the drone zipped around the yard and their tree.

"I remember that," Linden said. "The day we had the practice flights!"

The video skipped forward to the scene of the Bannon Foods warehouse. The auditorium grew hushed as they listened to the roar of the quadcopter's four rotors as it dove into the warehouse and dropped onto the tall dry-goods stack. The video played out in its entirety, the crowd gasping at times, quiet as others, laughing as it swooped to escape toward the end. When Mr. Hutchins downed the drone with the thrown broom there were outcries of anger and booing. Then the video ended, and the room lights came back up.

"Thanks to the scientific and detective work of Willow, Elon, and Linden we once again have the local, fresh, good food we were promised," Mrs. Winterson said. "You'll find them in the back row if you have any questions. Thank you and enjoy the science fair."

With a last squeal the microphone was silenced and the crowd turned and faced them at the back of the room.

"I wanna see," a kid yelled, and ran toward them. Within seconds, they had a crowd surrounding them.

CHAPTER TWENTY-THREE

On the Saturday morning after the science fair, Willow went to Atlanta's house. The human hair swing was set up in her backyard under a covered patio.

"It's a really good swing," Willow said. "It was a brilliant project."

"Thanks," Atlanta said. "It turns out that both of our projects were big hits at the science fair."

"It's funny how things worked out." Willow kicked higher. "You had the idea, but then got too sick for most of it. My brothers and I built an amazing drone, but it was destroyed before the fair."

"Things don't always work out the way you expect. Now it's my turn on the swing."

Willow jumped off, her feet skidding across the floor. "I'm really glad you're better."

"Me, too. Thanks for fixing the school lunches."

A few weeks passed, and they heard nothing about getting their drone back. One day, Mrs. Winterson called them into the office, and told them the trial would be starting the following week. Willow, Elon, and Linden would be called as witnesses.

The trial started on a Tuesday morning. They dressed up in their best clothes and their parents took them to the courthouse. Because they were supposed to be in school, the kids testified first in the morning, then had to go back to school.

Miss Berry and Mrs. Winterson were gone for three days, leaving the kids puzzled over what was happening. But on Friday morning, when they entered the cafeteria, Miss Berry was back behind the counter serving breakfast.

"Miss Berry, what happened?"

Miss Berry looked up from the tray of orange juice boxes she was putting out. "It turned out to be exactly as Elon had said in Mr. Bannon's office." She sighed and took a breath. "When Tom Bannon's father died and Tom inherited the business, he didn't know much about operating it. He testified that he depended on Mr. Hutchins, who had worked there for many years, to explain how things worked."

"And?" Willow said.

"The state lawyer investigated and found Mr. Hutchins hadn't had much money until about eight months ago. Then during the testimony it came out that Mr. Hutchins hadn't saved for retirement. What little he had was poorly invested. He wanted to retire, but couldn't. He started skimping on some of Bannon's smaller customers, but when we gave them the school contract for local food, Mr. Hutchins saw his opportunity to make even more. He was sure Tom wouldn't know enough to figure it out."

"I knew it!" Elon said.

"He also figured that kids wouldn't appreciate expensive food," Miss Berry said. "But he knew restaurants did. So he took the local foods that were supposed to be for Mt. Hood Elementary, and sold them to restaurants, without telling Mr. Bannon. The restaurants paid a lot of money, not knowing they were getting stolen food, and Mr. Hutchins kept it all."

"Where'd he get the food for our school?" Linden asked.

"Mr. Hutchins still needed to make the deliveries to hide his crime, so he looked around for really cheap food. He found a company in California that was selling excessed foods." Here Miss Berry swallowed deep, then continued in a whisper. "Food that were supposed to be served to farm animals because it wasn't good enough for people. He bought that junk, getting weekly deliveries in the early morning when no one else was around." She went back to a normal voice. "It was much cheaper than fresh food, so Mr. Hutchins was making thousands of dollars every week. For a long while no one had noticed. Until you three figured it out. Good job."

The bell rang, and the sound of six hundred kids running for class sounded out.

"Thanks, Miss Berry," Willow said as they ran to class.

That evening at home the phone rang.

"I got it," Elon yelled, running for the kitchen. "Hello?"

"Hi, it's Tom Bannon," the voice said.

"Hi, Mr. Bannon." Elon wasn't sure if Mr. Bannon would be angry. Was he in trouble?

"Mr. Hutchins is going to jail."

"I heard. I hope you're not in trouble," Elon said.

"No, no." There a soft chuckle from the other end of the line. "I actually wanted to say thank you. If it wasn't for you three, Mr. Hutchins could have gone on longer, more people would have gotten sick, and Bannon Foods and I could have gotten into bigger trouble. So I really appreciate you solving this mystery."

"You're welcome," Elon said.

"But the judge said I have to buy you kids a new drone. Will a thousand dollars cover it?"

Elon's eyes went big. A thousand dollars? They could build a supersized drone. But he didn't want to be dishonest. "It's too much, actually, Mr. Bannon. The first drone only cost about two hundred."

"Ah... Well, I'll send you a thousand dollars, and you can keep the rest as a reward."

Holy cow, a thousand dollars. Elon barely heard the rest of the conversation. Finally, after saying good-byes, he got off the phone and ran looking for the other kids.

"Willow, Linden, have I got some news!"

THE END

Dear Reader,

Thanks for buying *The Case of the Wilted Broccoli*. I hope you enjoyed it.

I'm an independent author. That means I don't have a big publishing company with a marketing department to help sell my books. I'm dependent on you, the reader, to tell others about my books.

If you like *The Case of the Wilted Broccoli*, please tell your friends or parents, ask a school library to carry it, or post a review online. Thank you!

Visit www.williamhertling.com if you'd like to learn more about my books, or subscribe to my monthly newsletter to find out when new books are released.

If you're looking for my books in stores, I write children's fiction under Will Hertling and books for adults and teens under William Hertling.

Sincerely,
Will Hertling

ACKNOWLEDGEMENTS

Thank you to my children for prompting me to write this novel, and continuing to remind me to work on it even as I was distracted by other projects, and for your patience.

Thank you to Erin Gately, as always, for your support: watching kids so I can write, reading and providing feedback, and general enthusiasm.

Thanks also to Maja Carrel Herrera for her support.

Thanks to the Wine Writers critique group for their incredibly helpful feedback on this and other projects: Catherine Craglow, Cathy Heslin, Shana Kusin, Amy Seaholt, and David Melville. Thanks also to Dr. Shana Kusin for medical advice.

Thank you to Maureen Gately, for your wisdom, knowledge and general excellence in all things design, print, and publishing related. I would be lost without your guidance.

Thanks to M.S. Corley for the cover design and illustration, Steve Bieler for copy editing, and Kiersi Burkhart for manuscript feedback.

Thank you to the kids who provided feedback: Abby, Ella, Gifford, Jake, Liam, Luc, Luka, Roland, and Rowan. Thanks also to their parents who helped with the process: Amelia, Brain, Dawn, Grace, Petar, Rebecca, and Brian. (Last names intentionally left out to protect their privacy.)

My apologies if I've missed anybody. Any errors that remain are my own.

About the Author

William Hertling is an award-winning science fiction writer, and the author of the *Singularity* series of novels for teens and adults: *Avogadro Corp.*, *A.I. Apocalypse*, and *The Last Firewall*.

A computer programmer and social media strategist, he lives in Portland, Oregon.

The Case of the Wilted Broccoli is his first novel for children.

To contact the author:
Web: www.williamhertling.com
Email: william.hertling@liquididea.com

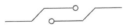

18990739R00097